MASTERMIND

BILLIONAIRES OF WHITE OAKS

LIZABETH SCOTT

And now it's my turn to save him,
From himself.

DUKE
I've never known anyone like her,
Gorgeous, smart, and slightly naïve,
But her sense of humor has me begging for more.
I'm drawn to her in ways I can't even explain.

Insisting she move in was my best decision,
And now, I'm getting to know Harlow in every way,
Feeling like she may be the Duchess to my Duke.

But I need to come clean about me,
Let her know the truth about me,
About my life.
Can a woman like her handle the secret I've been hiding?

**Each book in this steamy hot romantic series can be read
as a standalone, but for a richer reading experience, the
following order is recommended:**
  Heartbreaker – April & Elias
  Troublemaker – *Rachael & Kyle*
  Mastermind – Harlow & Duke
  Hothead – Baylee & Smith

Love at White Oaks

Heartbreaker

Troublemaker

Mastermind

Hothead

Love in Transit

Ticket to Forever

Ticket to Pleasure

Ticket to Desire

Connect with Liz on

Website: LizScottBooks.com

Facebook: LizabethScottAuthor

Twitter: @LScottBooks

Instagram: lizabethscottauthor

BookBub: bookbub.com/authors/lizabeth-scott

GoodReads:
goodreads.com/author/show/8122729.Lizabeth_Scott

For updates on releases, giveaways,

and special announcements

join my Newsletter Community by clicking
<u>HERE</u> or join by going to LizScottBooks.com

CHAPTER ONE

Harlow

"Hey, sugar. A pretty girl like you shouldn't be out walking all alone. Want me to give you a ride somewhere?" the man in a beat-up blue pickup asks as he slows to meet my pace.

That's not the first time I've heard that same offer today. I keep walking, but I turn my head. "No thanks. Just out for a walk." I give him a smile but don't slow down. I've learned that southerners are persistent.

"You sure?" he asks again.

"Oh yeah. But thanks for the offer." He glances at the toolbox in my hands, and I'm wondering if he's going to knock me over the head and take it or if he's just admiring the bling I decorated it with. Long after I can no longer smell his exhaust fumes, my stride hasn't changed. It would be so much easier to accept one of the many rides, but I've seen too many crime shows to trust that I would actually be delivered to my destination.

My stomach rumbles, my feet ache, and I'm so thirsty the nearby river is looking very tempting. I wipe the sweat from my brow and sigh. I hate to sweat. It's so gross, and I want to take a shower with my fuchsia-scented body wash, which I don't have. "Ugh!" I growl to the ants on the road.

I have nobody but myself to blame for my current no-car-no-money-no-nothing situation. I'm the one that believed my dad had changed. I'm the one that suggested we uproot our lives and move thousands of miles from the only place we'd ever called home.

It's hard to believe that my own father would ditch me in a hotel to chase after his next gambling fix. I'd only been gone fifteen minutes, just long enough to run across the road to get food. He didn't even leave my clothes. My feet stomp a little bit harder on the pavement I've been walking on for the past—oh, wait. I have no idea because I don't have my phone, either!

I decide to ignore my rumbling stomach because there's nothing I can do about it. All my money was hidden in the moving trailer that's attached to my car, which is who knows where. I have less than three hundred bucks left after paying for the hotel room, and I have to make it last until I can figure something out.

Finally, I walk past the Welcome to Treemont sign and

set my toolbox down on the side of the road and rub my cramped hand and back. Yeah, it's heavy and cumbersome, but I don't care. It's too precious to think of leaving behind just to make my load easier. I open the box, and the brightly colored beads and charms, perfectly organized by color and size, make me smile. In the compartments underneath, all my wire, silver, and tools are just waiting for me to create something pretty. My eyes sting, but I blink the tears away.

I want to believe Dad left them because he knows how much they mean to me. It's just a fishing tackle box filled with jewelry-making supplies, but it belonged to my mom. When I was little, she'd let me pick out my favorite beads, and I'd sit for hours watching her create something gorgeous with them. I close and lock the box and head toward the apartment complex I'd seen from the highway.

In the late afternoon, I limp into White Oaks, which turns out to be more like a town within a town. The six-story building must have been some type of factory mill at one time. Opposite the apartments, there's a brick-paved commons area with boutique shops, restaurants, and a specialty grocery store along the river's edge. Then there's a six-story, glass-and-brick building that completes the circle. The name on the outside of that building reads Ainsworth Enterprises.

I find a bench under a big oak tree to people-watch while I give my feet a rest. It's fascinating. There's no rushing or pushing. No loud traffic noises or yelling. Instead, two people are laughing outside of an art shop, and

I can hear birds jabbering in nearby trees. A grocer straightens one of his outside displays and stops to chat with a customer leaving. The bakery door opens, and a mother and her two daughters come out, each carrying a pink box of goodies. The sound of the river is relaxing, and the gentle breeze blowing across my face smells fresh and clean. I like it here.

I pick up my backpack and tackle box and head toward the shops, desperate for a drink of water. Hopefully, I'll find a water fountain. If not, I'll have to dip into my cash. A sign in the window of cute shop called Tea Thyme catches my eyes. I push through the door and am surrounded by a multitude of scents: cinnamon, oregano, basil, rosemary. The shop is actually divided into two stores. The left side is a tea shop, with shelves along the wall filled with tins of tea. Their names are listed on a small chalkboard in front of each. At the back of the store, a glass display case is filled with sweet treats like brownies, cookies, and cake pops. They smell so good that my mouth begins to water. Behind the display is the area where customers' drink orders are filled and a checkout area. The right side of the store is filled with wall-to-wall shelves and bins holding any type of herb or spice you could want. Some I don't even know how to pronounce. I turn when I hear steps.

"Sorry, I didn't hear you come in. Can I help you?"

I turn and find a young woman about my age walking toward me, wiping her hands on a towel as she comes through a door at the back of the store. She's cute, with her dark hair pulled into a ponytail, a pink-and-aqua polo shirt with the Tea Thyme logo stitched to the front, and black pants. She's shorter than my height of five foot seven inches, because I have to look down to say, "No problem. I've not been waiting. I saw your sign." I motion with my thumb over my shoulder.

Her already smiling face turns brighter as she asks, "Are you looking for work?"

I clear my parched throat, wishing I had found the water before coming inside. I nod and tell her, "I am."

She holds her hand out. "I'm the owner, Kaylee Conrad," she says.

I smile and shake her outstretched hand. "It's nice to meet you, Kaylee. I'm Harlow. Do you mind telling me about the job?"

"It's minimum wage, but there's a tip jar that's divided between whoever works that day. I can't give you many hours to start out, but when Leanne goes out on maternity leave—any minute now, if you ask me—I'll be able to use you full time. Have you ever done this type of work before?"

I flinch just a little and then push my shoulders back. I need this job, but I also want Kaylee to know the truth. "I've worked at a restaurant before as a waitress. I'll be honest, I wasn't very good at keeping orders straight."

Kaylee laughs and touches my arm. "Oh, don't worry about that, honey. This is nothing that busy. You'd have to learn our menu of teas and how to prepare them. We get all of our baked goods from a bakery in town, so there's nothing to learn there other than how to stock the display case. Does this sound like something you'd like?" she asks.

I nod and bite my lip, hoping she'll hire me. I could do this job. "Yeah. It does."

A big grin grows on her face. "When can you start?"

I can't help smiling back. She's infectious; she just has that type of personality. "I feel like if I say 'now,' it will make you very happy."

Kaylee chuckles. "We're going to get along just fine. How about you fill out the paperwork and come back in the morning? We open at six, but you'll need to be here at five-thirty. Let me fix you a glass of sweet tea and some of our treats to sample while you do that."

She doesn't know how perfect that sounds to me. I only hope she didn't hear my stomach growl.

As I'm filling out the papers, I look up when two very attractive women come in. Kaylee squeals when she sees them, and the three have a hug fest. I grin as they talk over each other and end up laughing at their silliness. I have a moment of longing. It would be incredible to have friends like that. I never had a chance to form friendships growing up; I'd been too busy working.

I finish the paperwork and eat every single one of the brownies Kaylee set down in front of me. After saying goodbye, I walk out of Tea Thyme feeling unsettled. What will I do for the night? Where can I go? I guess I could walk back to the hotel, but that would be another hundred bucks of my cash. The best I can hope for is to find someplace out of the way where I can have some seclusion. I follow the sidewalk and eventually end up in a park. There are swings, slides, and crawling gyms in a fenced-off section. My gaze lands on a covered tunnel at the top of the slides. It looks like I've found my accommodations for the night.

I'm back at Tea Thyme waiting for Kaylee when she drives up the next morning. It wasn't a fun night, and I'm not sure I closed my eyes at all. There were too many noises I couldn't explain, and I had to fold up my body to fit in the small space. I stretch and twist my back from side to side, trying to get all the kinks out. I've got to find something else. Fast. And I want a shower so bad I could cry.

"You're here bright and early," Kaylee greets me as she gets out of her car and walks around to the rear doors.

"Yeah, just excited to start," I tell her. As we round her van, a very colorful woman is busy pulling boxes from the back. Colorful because she has on orange pants and a pink Tea Thyme embroidered polo shirt with a big sunflower barrette in her hair. Somehow, the colors work on her.

"Harlow, this is my sister Baylee. She keeps a neighbor's daughter after school and helps around here sometimes."

I nod at the woman filling her arms with boxes from the van. "Hi, Baylee. It's nice to meet you." The two sisters are as different as night and day. Kaylee's hair is dark brown where Baylee's is light blond, and Kaylee is a few inches taller. Baylee looks like a sun-kissed fairy, and she makes me smile.

"Hey, Harlow," Baylee says. She drops the boxes and gives me a big hug. "Kaylee is so excited you're working here now. I know we're going to be great friends," she tells me as her hug continues.

Her hazel eyes sparkle, and I feel a bit uncomfortable. Over-friendly much? "That's great." I never knew that a face could actually light up, but that's exactly what Baylee's did. I grab some of the boxes.

"Well, come on in and let's have a cup of tea before we get started." Kaylee says, and we head to the back door. She balances three boxes in her arms while she fishes around in her bag for the key to unlock the door.

I've never been a tea drinker, so the whole process is foreign to me. After we unload the inventory, Kaylee shows me how to work the machines to prepare a cup. After a few questions for clarification, I try, and the little tag on the tea bag falls inside the cup. "Oh no!"

Kaylee chuckles, "Don't worry. That happens all the time. Just dig it out with one of these." She holds up a disposable stirrer. "Then tuck it into the lip of the cup," she demonstrates.

We sit at one of the tables out front with our tea and sweets while Baylee is in the kitchen, singing loudly and off key, but it doesn't seem to bother her. I chuckle and check out today's treat, a big fat juicy cinnamon bun that I want to devour.

"So, I saw on your paperwork you're from New Jersey," Kaylee asks, keeping an eye on her sister as she carries a tray of sweets from the back and starts to fill the display case.

Nervously, I tuck my shoulder-length blonde hair behind my ear and answer, "That's right." I take a sip of tea and stuff half the bun in my mouth, hoping she won't ask any more questions. I didn't want to lie to her, but I also can't have her find out about my living conditions. Kaylee is so sweet. I know she'd help me out, and that's exactly why I don't want her to know. It's embarrassing enough. I'm not really sure what the deal is with Baylee, but Kaylee keeps watch over her like a mother hen, ready to swoop in if needed.

"Your sister is really sweet," I say as I break off another piece of the most delicious cinnamon bun I've ever eaten. First the spicy smell gets my taste buds all excited, then the burst of sugar and cinnamon explodes on my tongue, and the pastry is so soft it almost melts in my mouth.

Kaylee chuckles. "By the look on your face I think you like the bun."

I smile and wipe my mouth before admitting, "It's divine."

Her gaze moves back to her sister, and she smiles, "Yes. Baylee is very special. She can be a bit over-friendly at times—well, most of the time—but she's just a genuinely caring person." Kaylee lowers her voice and leans closer. "Listen, never let Baylee behind the register."

Our eyes meet, and I can see how much it bothers her to say that. I can't believe that sweet and innocent woman would steal money from her sister. "Okay…" I draw my confirmation out, hoping she'll elaborate, but she doesn't. Kaylee is a new friend, but she's also my boss, so I don't ask.

I feel like she wants to say more, but instead we talk about Treemont and some of the duties I'll be doing while we finish our tea. Then we set up the tables for customers, finish filling the display case with fresh-baked goods, and Baylee flips the *Closed* sign to *Open*.

"Look!" Baylee shouts and shoots out the door, calling over her shoulder, "I'll be right back."

Kaylee looks up from filling the till for the day and laughs, nodding in the direction she ran. "That's Mr. Wilton with Mr. Boots. Baylee loves dogs."

I watch her drop to her knees and hug the tiny Yorkie, who covers her face with doggie kisses. I have to laugh at the sight. Then she holds the pup's face in her hands like she's talking right to him. She looks up and says something to the gentleman, then her whole body droops. When she returns, it's obvious something is upsetting her.

"What's wrong, Bay?" Kaylee asks.

I honestly think her eyes are filling with tears. Did she find out someone died? Instead, Baylee says, "Mr. Boots is miserable. Ms. Wilton has been working longer hours lately, and Mr. Boots doesn't like staying home alone."

What? Slowly, I turn my head to Kaylee curious to see her reaction. Our eyes meet, and she shrugs and says, "I'm sorry, Bay."

Baylee sighs dramatically. "I wish there was something I could do," she says. Then she walks to the back, her shoulders slumped in despair.

Kaylee is right. Baylee really likes dogs.

CHAPTER TWO

Harlow

Towards the middle of the afternoon, I have my first solo customer of the day. He's a very striking man in a dark-gray suit. By *striking*, I mean drool may be seeping from the corners of my mouth. I can't look away. I know I'm being incredibly rude, but I've never seen anyone as handsome. Buddy from the garage I used to work at holds the previous title, and he's usually covered in grease and has a receding hairline.

I tip my head in deep thought as he approaches the counter, trying to decide if he looks more like Andrew Lincoln or Ryan Gosling. His hair's darker like Andrew's, but his chin's strong like Ryan's. And that suit... I sigh.

Dreaminess. Who knew I liked a man in a well-fitting suit? Completely swoon-worthy. And I feel dirty but not in a good way. I wish I had clean hair and at least a little lipstick. Then he speaks, and my insides go all aflutter.

"Good day. I'd like a cup of Earl Grey, please. Cream and sugar," he says, and I want to ask him to repeat his order just to hear him speak again. His voice is reserved and deeply English. Very English.

His dark hair is styled impeccably. Short and neat, with longer tresses on top, and all I want to do is run my fingers through and mess it up. There's no stubble to mar his perfect features. I grip the edge of the counter to keep from reaching out to discover exactly how smooth and soft his skin feels. I look up to find smoky-blue eyes staring into mine before I realize I've been daydreaming about the man, the customer, that's waiting for his tea.

"Certainly, sir. I'll get that for you." I prepare his tea after I fish the darn tag out and ring him up while continuing to sneak peeks. I put the cup cozy on and hand it to him with a big smile. "Here you go."

"Thank you," he says as he takes the cup from my hands. Our fingers brush. A zap of electric energy causes his eyes to flash to mine with a startled look. He felt it, too. I'm glad he took possession of the hot liquid, because my hand and arm suddenly don't feel as if they belong to me. "Sorry about that. Static electricity," I give as a hopeful excuse.

"Of course," he says, accepting my explanation. Because what else could it be?

"Have a great day," I mumble as he turns to leave.

I follow his route as he leaves the shop. I frown when he takes one sip of his tea, grimaces, and tosses the rest in a trash can as he passes. That's weird. I know I made it correctly. He disappears inside the Ainsworth building across the commons area. He must be an executive. Another customer comes in, and that's my last thought of Mr. Earl Grey.

The rest of the day goes by fast, and I've been trying to come up with a plan for the night. All day long I've been watching people go in and out of White Oaks apartments. I could probably slip inside and find some out-of-the-way place to sleep. Maybe under a stairwell? That has to be safer than sleeping out in the open park.

When my shift is over, I time it just right so I follow a couple into the apartment complex before the door locks behind them. I don't stop at the first floor. That would be too easy to be discovered. I ride up in the elevator to the second floor and walk the halls from one side to the other without finding anything even remotely feasible. I go back to the elevator and go up one level. There I discover the entire third floor of the old cotton mill has not yet been renovated. I find everything has been gutted down to bare studs. Almost in the middle of the building I find what might have once been an office or supply room that has been left intact with its four walls and even a door. Maybe the contractor's plan was to store supplies and tools in the room during the renovation. I'm not sure, but it's my lucky day. I unpack my backpack and hang my one extra pair of jeans and t-shirt from nails I find in the walls. Probably where pictures once hung. Thank goodness my new job comes with uniforms. That night I fall asleep as I sit on the floor, leaning against the wall. I wonder where my dad is and if he's safe. I say a prayer and then fall into an exhausted sleep, but not before I remember the touch of Mr. Earl Grey.

The next morning, I wake up with another stiff neck and a sore back. I'll need to find something to use as a bed. Even a blow-up water float would be better. I could probably find one of those cheap at a Dollar Store—if I knew where one was.

That afternoon, I look up from cleaning a teapot, and my heartrate spikes when the delicious man from yesterday walks into the shop. Again, I'm struck by his gorgeousness. I purse my lips in thought. *Andrew Lincoln, for sure.*

"Good day. I'd like a cup of Earl Grey. Cream and sugar," he says sharply and begins drumming his fingers on the counter.

My eyes go to his well-manicured hands. "Right away." I want to believe he's as nice as he looks, so I overlook his annoying beat. It's not going to make the water heat any faster. *"Darn!"* The tag falls inside the cup. I fish it out with a stirrer and add the cream and sugar. Stir and cap the cup. I've got this.

Today when our hands touch, I'm ready for the impact. Or at least I thought I was. The warm glow still makes my

LIZABETH SCOTT

hand and arm tingle. "Um, enjoy your tea." I smile and wish he'd stay a bit longer.

"That's yet to be determined," he replies and turns to leave.

"Well, have a lovely afternoon," I call to his retreating back. He pauses with a perplexed look on his face like that small pleasantry is foreign to him. He nods. I almost expect to hear his heels click. "I noticed you going into the Ainsworth building. Is that where you work?"

He checks his watch before answering. I know nothing about men's watches, but that one looks very expensive. "That's correct, and I'm running late. If you'll excuse me…"

I can take a hint, so I don't say anything else. Instead I watch him cross the commons area, in his brisk, determined stride. Again, he takes a sip of his tea, his face turns up in disgust just before he tosses the perfectly prepared cup of tea in the trash. I may have to rethink my attraction to him. He looks like he could be a happy person…with a lot of work. Somehow, I think it would be very rewarding to take on that task.

That night after work, as I sneak into White Oaks, a very sweet-looking yet strange woman catches me before I get on the elevator. She's wearing a lime-green track suit that went out with the eighties, and her snow-white hair is in a messy ponytail on top of her head. I actually have to do a double-take, then I wonder if she's on her way to a costume party.

16

"Excuse me, dear. I don't believe we've met. I'm Ms. Edna from 1A."

She smiles and I find myself smiling back. "It's nice to meet you. I'm Harlow, and I'm working over at Tea Thyme." I hope she doesn't ask which apartment I'm in.

"Oh, that's wonderful. I'm sure Kaylee is glad to have you. You know, I was on my way to the recycling bins, but I wonder if you'd have a need for some old quilts? Blanche and I were cleaning out some closets today, and I can't believe how much junk we've accumulated over the years. It's rather disgraceful, if you ask me. Blanche can't throw anything away."

I eye the large cardboard box at her feet. Why would she offer them to me? She's never even met me before. It's almost like she... *No. There's no way.* "I don't know..."

"It would save me a trip outside if you'd take them. Plus, I know with just moving in, things can get misplaced until you're unpacked," she says with wink and a twinkle in her eyes.

My eyes narrow, feeling like I've never received the memo. She's waiting for my answer, and I somehow feel played. But, no. What am I even thinking? This kind woman doesn't have an agenda, and it would be nice to have something soft to sleep on. My back still has a kink in it from last night. "Well, sure. I'd be happy to take them. Thank you."

"Oh, that's wonderful. Well, I've got to run. I left a pie in the oven. Stop by sometime and meet Blanche. Maybe even come for dinner one night." She turns, and with a spring in her step, she leaves.

"That would be nice, Ms. Edna. Thank you," I call to her quickly retreating back.

When I get upstairs with the big box, I have to wonder how Ms. Edna got the heavy thing to the elevator. She must be a lot stronger than she looks. I can't believe my luck when I open the box and find four incredible handmade quilts. Surely, they didn't make them? But I bet they did. I can't believe they were going to just toss them away. In the bottom of the box, I find a fluffy feather pillow, a flashlight with an extra pack of batteries, and half a dozen very racy romance novels, if the covers are anything to go by. I laugh at the men's bare, bulging chests and the heaving bosoms of the scantily dressed women on the covers and can't believe that little old lady could handle a book this steamy. At the very bottom of the box, I find a one-piece swimsuit that looks like something straight from the eighties, and a campus map of White Oaks. I turn it over in my hand and move to the windows so I can see it better, using the outside flood lights.

I never realized the complex was so large. There's even an indoor pool, a gym, and a spa on the sixth floor with locker room accommodations. Maybe I could take a shower or even get in the spa. That would feel so good on my aching muscles. Without giving too much thought about how wrong it is, I grab the bathing suit and get back on the elevator, and this time I push six. When I get off, I follow the signs to the women's locker room. I find a dozen indi-vidual shower stalls and a centralized locker room with benches and stacks of white cotton towels. I change into my bathing suit—or rather, Ms. Edna's bathing suit—and follow the signs to the spa. I turn the doorknob slowly and peek into the room. At first, I don't see anyone, and I take a tentative step inside. Then I see two heads pop up from inside the hot tub. I try to back out of the room, but then one of the ladies motions for me to come over. When I'm closer, I see it's the two women I'd seen when I was filling out my paperwork.

"Hi, my name is April," the first woman calls out.

The second woman smiles and waves as she says, "And I'm Rachael."

If I join them, this could blow everything. They may pick right up on the fact that I don't belong here. But they've already seen me. It's too late now. I straighten my sore back and smile back at them while I ask, "Hey, do you mind if I join you?"

"No, come on in." April says.

I pull my purple-tipped hair into a high bun to keep it away from the chlorine and climb in. I suppose I'll just let the coloring wash out. There's no way I can afford to keep it up.

Once I'm seated and the warm water is swirling around me, I introduce myself. "I'm Harlow. Nice to meet you."

"You work over at the tea shop, don't you?" Rachael asks.

"Yeah," I say, intentionally keeping my answer short.

"Do you live here, in the complex?" April asks.

"Um, yeah," I say, again with the one-word answers. I see them glance at each other, probably agreeing that I'm acting strange. I glance toward the door. Maybe I should just leave.

"Do you have any family that moved with you?" Rachael asks.

I look down at the bubbly water. I don't want to lie, so I answer, "No. It's just me."

"Have you been here long?" April asks.

I glance at the two curious women and smile, knowing this time I have no option but to lie. "No, not too long. Just a few weeks." If I tell them I've only been here a few days that would only create more questions I don't want to answer.

Rachael asks. "Where are you from?"

I pause before answering vaguely. "Up north in New Jersey."

April asks, "So, do you like it here?"

"It's different, but yeah, I really do like it. The people are nice, and I love my job with Kaylee at Tea Thyme. Who knew there were so many different types of tea?" That was the truth.

"We love Kaylee, too. Hey, that's a really cute bracelet you have on."

I hold up my arm and glance at the purple and clear

quartz bracelet. The color combination had been a happy accident. "Thanks."

Rachael asks, "Where did you find it? I'd like to get one for my son's grandmother."

I look up at them, stunned, unable to believe she'd want one. "I...um, I made it."

April and Rachael both say at the same time, "You did?"

"You're really good," April says. "Where do you sell your pieces?"

I shrug. "Oh, I don't. But if you want, I can make your son's grandmother one," I offer.

"That would be wonderful." Rachael says, seeming genuinely excited.

"I want one too." April says. "I really think you need a webpage. I can talk to a friend about creating you one if you'd like."

"I'll be happy to make you a bracelet too," I tell them. Then I shake my head. "But I don't want a webpage. At least not yet. Maybe someday." These ladies are incredible.

"Well, you just let me know when you're ready, and I'll make it happen," April says.

I give them both a smile and quickly say, "You both are very kind. Thank you."

"You know," Rachael says, "since you're new to the area, we should get together and do something."

April's eyes light up. "That's a great idea. We can show her around and introduce her to folks. I have a feeling Banks would love to meet you. Do you have a boyfriend?"

My eyes grow huge, and I stumble in answering. "N-no."

"Banks would be perfect for her," Rachael agrees.

"Hold on." I say, with what I know must be a look of horror on my face. "I don't want—"

Rachael snaps her fingers and interrupts. "Or how about one of your brothers?" She turns to me and explains, "April has three incredibly handsome brothers. You should invite Harlow over on the next barbeque night, April! Harlow, give me your number, and I'll give you a call."

I've got to get out of here before they have me married off! I stand up abruptly, sloshing water over the sides, and give them both a frantic smile before stepping over the side and saying, "Well, I need to go now. It was nice meeting you both." I climb from the water and almost sprint for the door.

Later that night, I'm sitting on the soft blankets, with my toolbox in front of me, working on a design I've been thinking about since I made my first cup of tea and that silly tag fell in the cup. I hold up my efforts and smile. I think this will work nicely. It's very simple, really. Just a jewelry clasp that I've added a gemstone and a charm to. I think it has enough weight to it to keep the tag from falling in the cup. I'll clip it to the tea tag before pouring in the water, and if it works as I think, I'll never have to fish out another tag. Before I go to bed that night, I've made several dozen of what I've decided to call Tea Charms.

The next morning as I walk in the door at work, I hear

them before I see them. It's April talking to Kaylee. I can't imagine why April is here so early.

"Harlow," Kaylee says as the women walk over to me. "This is April Holt, one of my best friends."

I smile at them and say, "Hey again." Then I turn to Kaylee, "We've already met. Last night in the hot tub. I met April and Rachael."

"Ah, yes. Before the drama." Kaylee says.

My brows pinch together, "Drama?" I ask.

Both women nod, and then April explains, "Rachael is Kyle Welsh's baby mama, and the media got wind of that secret and mobbed her house."

My mouth drops open in shock. "Kyle Welsh as in Filthy Arc?" I ask to clarify we're both talking about the lead singer of the most popular band in the world.

April grins. "That would be the one. I stopped by to take her and her son, Henry, some comfort food while she's confined to her house."

"Wow…" is all I'm able to say.

"I know, right? He's hot off the charts. But if you tell my husband I said that, I will deny it." April laughs, but she's dead serious.

Kaylee shakes her head at her friend's comment then says, "Harlow is going to be working for me part-time until Leanne has the baby."

"I hope you don't have another job in mind, because I bet once the baby's born, Leanne will decide to stay home."

Kaylee nods in agreement. "She was probably only

working here to help me out, so it wouldn't surprise me. Let me pack some things up for you to take to Rachael."

"Hey, that's a beautiful necklace you have on. Did you make that too?" April asks, and my hand flies to my neck.

"Oh, yeah. I made it." I pull on the beads nervously. It's okay, but it's still an amateur attempt. I'd used blue sea glass beads of varying sizes and formed twisted wire connectors attached to an antique bronze chain.

April reaches out and fingers the beads around my neck. "You did?" she asks. "It's gorgeous. You really need a shop. Or at least sell them online."

"Oh, no. I just play around with making things. I don't sell them." I'm still awestruck that I've met someone that knows Kyle Welsh.

"Well, you should," April says.

I shrug, "I don't know. I don't imagine anyone would buy them." I give most of my attempts away to neighbors and co-workers. They seem to like them, but I doubt they would have been interested in purchasing any.

April shocks me when she says, "I have this blue dress and something like you're wearing would go perfect."

Without a second thought, I take off my necklace and hand it to her. "Here, you can have this one."

April's eyes grow large right along with her mouth. "Really? You'll let me have this one? Are you sure? I'll pay you for it," she offers.

I grin at her excitement but shake my head. "No." As

much as I need the money, I don't even consider accepting anything from her. "It's a gift."

Her eyes go bright and she asks, "Do you make earrings to match?"

Is she really interested in my jewelry, or is she simply being nice? At this point, I don't know her well enough to decide. "I guess I could."

I'm stunned when April says, "You know, you can bring them the next time we have a girl's night. In fact, bring everything you have made up so we can all shop."

"You want me to join you and your friends?" I ask, concerned I've misunderstood. They just met me.

April grins and says. "Sure. You can be a newly-elected member of our group. We all used to live here at White Oaks before I got married and Rachael moved in with Kyle. We've all grown up together since kindergarten. There's not much we don't know about the area and each other."

Kaylee hands April a pink box of delicious-smelling goodies and says, "You're new to town, and we can be your guides to all that is Treemont and White Oaks. I definitely want in on your jewelry designs. Sorry, I've been listening in. I noticed your necklace as soon as you walked in."

How it happened, I don't actually know, but I know I've found my new home.

After a week at work, I feel like I'm catching on. I've even chatted with a few customers. Mr. Hawkins is a farmer and runs a farmer's market on Tuesdays and Thursdays at the town square. He promised me a basket of apples if I stop by. And Angie Wright has a hair and nail salon on Main Street, and she gave me a coupon for a free cut and style. My purple tips are fading, but they simply have to go. Everyone I've met in Treemont is so nice. Everybody but one, that is. When I see Mr. Earl Grey walking across the commons area, I go ahead and start making his tea. He's been in every day, and his tea always ends up in the trash.

Smiling, I greet him as he walks in. "Good morning." Then I hold out his perfectly prepared cup of tea. I will be nice no matter how grumpy he is.

"What's this?" he asks and looks like I'm handing him a cup of poison.

I smile sweetly and say, "Earl Grey, cream and sugar. Would you like for me to go ahead and dump it in the trash for you?"

His eyes move from my hand holding the offered cup to my eyes, and I swear I see a flicker of amusement in them. "I meant this dangly thing," he says as he hands me a five-dollar bill.

I look up from making his change. "Oh, sorry. I forgot and left that on there." I reach to take the cup back, but he holds it out of my reach.

He fingers the charm, studying it closely, and I bite my lip nervously. "What is it?" he asks again.

"Just something I made to keep the tea tag from falling inside the cup," I say and feel a blush rising on my face.

His eyes draw together and a grin threatens to form on his face. "You have a problem with that?" he asks.

I grin and tuck my hair behind my ear before admitting, "Yeah. I do."

Again, he examines the tiny charm. "And you made it?"

I nod and wish he'd stop making a big deal out of it.

"This is a very creative and innovative design. You should do well selling them. Do you have a marketing plan?"

I can't help it. I laugh out loud, startling several customers. "No. I don't have one of those. They're just a silly little thing that helps me out. Kaylee said I could use them, and that's all I'm concerned with." Actually, Kaylee loved them and wanted me to make a few dozen to sell in the store.

"If you change your mind, I'll help you put a plan together."

I meet his gaze and nod. I mean, how ridiculous could he be? I don't even know how to respond to that, so I change the subject instead. "Why do you buy a cup of tea when you only throw it away?" I ask.

"Oh, you've seen that, have you?" He pulls at his tie as if he's uncomfortable about having been caught.

"It's hard to miss," I reply, and he gives me a small upward pull of his lips. I wouldn't call it a smile, but it wasn't his usual smirk. I count that as progress.

"American tea is rather different from what I'm used to. I keep hoping to acquire a taste for it, but it hasn't occurred as of yet," he says with a tinge of sadness.

"How long have you been trying?" I ask.

"I've lived here off and on for about ten years, but as for coming into this shop specifically, one week and three days."

Our eyes meet, and I feel a twinge in the area between my legs. An area that's been twinge-less for so long, I can't even remember.

That's strange. That's the exact number of days that I've been working here. Wait. What I'm thinking is crazy. No. He couldn't be coming because of me. No way. But still… "My name is Harlow."

"You may call me Duke," he says, as if it's a royal decree.

I laugh, "As opposed to…" I wait for him to answer.

His eyes widen, and then the corners crinkle as he fights a grin that eventually wins. "You're a funny lady, Harlow."

His grin makes my stomach do flips, and it totally transforms his face. "You're a very serious man, Duke."

"I'm not that serious. It's a British thing," he says, but I don't buy it.

I cross my arms, on a mission to make him admit he's too serious. I notice his eyes go to my chest and I quickly uncross my arms. "What do you wear when you get home from work?" I ask with all seriousness.

His brow rises and he asks, "Is this a trick question?"

I give my head an exaggerated shake back and forth. "Just answer the question."

He looks up in thought before meeting my gaze once

again and saying, "My suit, of course. Why would I change?"

I doubt he needed time to think about that. "Mm-hmm, and what do you do on your days off?"

This time he doesn't pause before answering. "I work. I don't have time to take days off. And speaking of work, I need to get back to it, but it's been lovely chatting."

"I rest my case." I laugh and say, "Do you want me to just bring your tea over tomorrow so you don't have to stop work? I mean all that fresh air you get between here and there must be so horrible for you."

He pauses and turns back with an actual smile on his handsome face. It makes him look years younger. "You know, that's not a bad idea. Actually, it's perfect. I'll make arrangements with Ms. Conrad later today."

He leaves me scratching my head, wondering what he meant and what I'm doing flirting with a man like Duke. A few minutes before my shift is over, Kaylee finds me wiping down tables, and I can tell from the pleased yet smug look on her face that something is up.

"Well, somebody made an impression," she says with a teasing light in her eyes.

I give her a clueless look and ask, "What are you talking about?"

"The owner of the apartment complex and Ainsworth Enterprises wants you to start bringing his tea to his office at three o'clock sharp." She winks, and I have no idea what she means.

"What? Who?" *A personal delivery?*

"Duke Ainsworth. He called and asked for you specifically. He's even going to be sending a tea service for you to use." She waggles her brows at me.

"What's a tea service?" I ask.

She shrugs and pulls out her phone. "I didn't know either. I had to Google it. Look." She holds up her phone, and I see a silver tray holding a fine china teapot, cups and saucers, a little covered dish for sugar, and a small pitcher for the cream. "He's even going to overnight his favorite Twinings tea from England."

"Oh my gosh! Why?" I'm excited and I'm terrified. Why would he do this? That's really going to the extreme for a cup of tea.

"I would think maybe someone has made an impression. Is there something going on between you two?" She leans back, waiting for me to answer.

I shake my head. "No, of course not. I mean, I think he's handsome. And, well, he does look nice in his suits, but we've shared nothing more than a few conversations."

Her lip rises like she doesn't believe me. "Well, honey, you did something. I've never seen him come out of his glass tower to visit with the small people before, so something is drawing him here. Now, go home. Your shift is over."

As I leave, I'm so lost in thought that I almost trip over something as I'm going by the recycling dumpsters. I look down and can't believe my luck. *A lamp!* I just hope it works or that I can figure out how to fix it. I bend down and pick up the cardboard box holding a very pretty blue-and-white porcelain lamp with a white shade, and I spot a box of lightbulbs as well. Double score!

I look around to see if someone is coming back for it. Who would have tossed something this nice? I see a neon pink flash of fabric going inside the doors. Could Ms. Edna have left this here? I wait around for about ten minutes, and when a young couple goes in the building, I sneak in behind them.

When I get to my room and hook up the lamp, I squeal when it works. I'll make a point to check the dumpster every day.

The next day, dressed in my regulation Tea Thyme polo shirt and black pants, I carefully carry the beautiful tea service across the commons area. Kaylee said to ride the elevator to the third floor. The bell dings, and I step out into a beautifully decorated foyer. Everything is sleek and modern, yet it fits the old building's atmosphere perfectly. The floors are wide-plank wood and are finished to a whiteoak tone. The outer walls are floor-to-ceiling windows, and two of the inner walls are left showing the natural antique brick.

"You must be Harlow."

I shift my eyes to one of the brick walls, where a smiling

older woman sits behind a desk, with a headset on. She's wearing a fuchsia suit jacket. Her light brown hair has only a few wisps of gray and is swept up into an elegant twist behind her head. "Yes, ma'am. I've brought Mr. Ainsworth's tea."

"Of course," she says, and her eyes go to my neck. "I can't help noticing that's a lovely necklace you're wearing. Where ever did you find it? My granddaughter would love something like that."

"Um, I didn't buy it. I made it." I sit the tray down on the corner of her desk and take my necklace off. "Here, you can give her this one."

Her eyes grow big, and she shakes her head. "No, dear. I didn't mean for you to give me yours. Make me one, and I'll gladly pay you for it."

"No, really. Take this one. I can always make more," I insist.

She holds up a finger and then points to her headset to let me know she has an incoming call. "Yes, sir. She just arrived. I'm sending her in now." She points to the door behind her. I lay the necklace on her desk, pick up the tray, and follow her. Evidently, Mr. Ainsworth doesn't like to be kept waiting.

Before I even set the service down, he says, "You're late."

"And you're still grouchy," I counter with a raised brow. "Where do you want this? It's heavy."

"There." He points to a small table in front of a charmingly decorated sitting area with a couch and two chairs. When I straighten up, Duke is behind me, and I jump. "Oh, I didn't see you." He steadies me with a hand on my elbow, and I may have leaned into him.

"Sorry, but did you expect me to drink my tea from behind my desk?" he asks with an innocent grin.

My stomach sinks from his nearness. "Well, I guess not. But give a girl a warning next time." I take a few side steps so I can breathe.

"So noted. Please sit." He motions to the couch behind me.

I take another side step. "No, I can't stay. I have to get back to work."

He gives me an arched brow. "I've already cleared it with Ms. Conrad. You'll stay, and I'll teach you to pour a proper tea."

"Mr. Ain…" I try to argue with him, but then he looks at me all dashingly charming, and I'm lost.

"Duke. Remember? Please, call me Duke. Now, let's get started." He rubs his hands together and smiles. "The trick to a perfect cup of tea is…"

CHAPTER THREE

Duke

"Really, Mum, I've already said I'd be home for the wedding," I say, motioning for my assistant to go to the next correspondence that needs my attention. She hands me a contract, and I skim through it while listening to my mother on speaker phone go on about the obnoxious wedding I'm required to attend.

I flip to page two and answer my mother's question at the same time. "Right. I won't be late. I'll be there a day early on the fourteenth. I've already notified the pilot of my return home."

Everything looks in order. I pick up my Montblanc, a gift from Her Majesty upon my graduation from Oxford, and sign my name before handing the papers off to Ms. Sheldon, who promptly replaces them with another document.

My mother has now moved on to the Wickhams, and were my life to depend upon it, I could not say what evil deed they'd done now. But the Breckenridge merger I'm reviewing has been updated to include the replacement of their staff, should they prove inadequate. My name goes neatly on the line indicated by the red sticky arrow. I hand this one off as well, pleased that I've been able to move through the entire stack while Mum natters on.

I check the time and see we've been chatting for close to an hour. "So sorry, Mum. I must ring off now." A few moments later, I disconnect the call, and Ms. Sheldon gives me a stern look of reproach for cutting my mum short. I have not one bit of remorse. I know my mum's ability to wax on for hours about nothing. "What?" I ask, and her brow rises almost into her hairline. I shrug, "She would have gone on for another hour if I hadn't cut her off."

One corner of her mouth curls into a grin. "Yes, sir. Is there anything else I can do for you?"

My lips thin at her insolence, but what am I to do? We both know she's the one who runs things around here. That's why I can spend as much time in England as I do and not worry about everything falling apart.

When I'm on this side of the pond, I leave all the trappings of my position in the UK. There are precisely two bespoke suits in my closet for emergencies, and the rest, as the Americans say, are business casual. I even have several pair of dungarees, which I quite enjoy, and those horrible shirts with snaps instead of buttons. Snaps! As if I were in bloody knickers.

"No, that will be all for now." I frown at her retreating back. All because I didn't let Mum talk my ear off. "Wait." Ms. Sheldon pauses at the door, her pen at the ready to note my request. "Please send Harlow right in when she gets here."

Her all-too-knowing eyes glance up from her empty pad with a smug grin in place on her face. "Right away, sir. I'll be sure to send her in when she gets here, promptly at three o'clock, like she's been doing for months now." She closes the door behind her with a decidedly loud click.

I frown at her cheekiness. I give it ten minutes before I station myself at the wall of windows overlooking the commons area below my office. When the door to the tea shop opens, my heart beats a bit faster in anticipation of seeing Harlow. Right on time, she comes out the door, walking quickly yet cautiously across brick pavers, carrying my silver service. When she reaches this side of the brick patio, I can no longer see her, but I know she's taking the elevator up.

Quickly, I return to my desk, waiting for her to enter. Every day I spend with her is another day spent getting to know her, and it's one more day that I must mask my feelings of wanting to make her mine. It's becoming increasingly hard. I rub my forehead and shift uncomfortably in my seat, regretting that choice of words. She's completely wrong for me, yet I look forward to our daily meetings. Harlow is truly the most interesting woman I've ever met. I don't know if I'm happy or sad that she's never accepted any of my invitations over the months I've known her. I finally stopped asking.

She walks through the door, with a fixed focus on not dropping the tray. Her pretty pink tongue peeks from the left corner of her lips. "Here's your order. Right on time, just how you like," she says, but as always, I have to give my body time to adjust to Harlow. It's been that way since the first time I saw her sitting on a bench below my window. Her purple hair had drawn my attention first, and when she'd gone into the tea shop, I had to follow her. Then, like a sap, I'd gone back day after day, until she'd suggested we have tea in my office.

She glances down at the tea tray she was still balancing and corrects herself. "Can I set this down, Duke, before I drop it all over your fancy rug?"

My lips twitch as I nod my approval, not even correcting her grammar, and I motion for her to begin our afternoon tea. *Duke.* I wish she would call me by my actual name. Or any of my real names, Oliver Alexander Phillip Ainsworth. Duke is my title, not my name when I'm home in England. But here in America, what started as a misunderstanding has become a nickname of sorts—which I don't correct. I much prefer the casualness and anonymity the moniker provides.

I follow Harlow with my eyes as she places the silver

service on the table, rattling the fine china a bit. I fight back a grin at the sulky expression on her face before she sits. I find that a practice I often must do in her presence. She thinks it's improper to address me as such and to take tea with me while she's working. I've discussed this with her boss, another thing she didn't appreciate. Eventually, we reached an understanding of sorts.

"Shall I pour?" she asks properly and waits for me to indicate she may.

Her graceful hands prepare the teacups by warming them with a splash of hot water from the teapot. She swirls and discards the water in a bowl before placing my favorite Twinings tea in each china cup and filling them slowly with hot—not boiling—water. She flips the egg timer over for a three-minute steep. Perfect. Just the way I've taught her.

Today her fingernails are polished a pretty neon-pink shade which goes nicely with her purple tipped hair. My eyes narrow on her swinging hair. The purple is almost faded out. I rather miss the vibrant color. While her choice of expression would be scandalous in my circle back in England, I find I love the avant-garde look. Harlow is fascinating and so vastly different from anyone I know.

"Where are we in our discussion?" I note the interest in her eyes, and I'm pleased she finds enjoyment in our book studies. I watch as she spreads strawberry jam on a scone. I sigh, wishing there were a dollop of clotted cream on top.

She hands me a china plate with one of the prepared

scones. "We were talking about the symbolism of Mr. Rochester losing his hand and sight."

I lean back in my chair and tent my fingers. "Ah, yes. Thornfield burning. And your impression?"

She picks up her china plate and slides back in the chair to get comfortable for our chat. "Well, I think it's a turning point for Mr. Rochester," she says before taking a bite of her scone. I watch her gleaming white teeth slice neatly through the confection. A crumb is left behind on her bottom lip, and her delicate pink tongue slips out and swipes it away. I pull at my tie to loosen it a bit as the room suddenly seems uncomfortably hot.

I nod my agreement and prompt her, "Go on." She chews slowly, thinking of her answer. I love the way her blue eyes shine as she tries to formulate her words. When I discovered her lack of knowledge of the classics, I set about tutoring her. I loan her a book from my own library to read, then we discuss during our afternoon tea. This month has been *Jane Eyre* by Charlotte Brontè. I've found Harlow to be a quick study and intelligent in her interpretation.

She takes a moment to collect her thoughts. "He wanted to change his wild, impulsive ways, but he couldn't. I think he wanted to be the kind of man Jane deserved."

I set my cup down on its saucer soundlessly. "Not necessarily that he felt she deserved it. He used Jane's goodness as an impetus to his transformation into a better man."

She nods, and her eyes glaze over. "Change is hard. Even with the best of intentions, the lure of old temptations can become too hard to resist. Mr. Rochester tried to change but couldn't until he lost everything he held dear."

Her response doesn't exactly address the scene in discussion, but I feel she's speaking on a more personal level. In fact, I wonder if she's still in the room with me. Our conversations have never taken a personal turn, and I want to ask her what, in her past, has put that sorrowful look on her face. I would like to make that look go away. "It was only after his loss of hand and sight that Mr. Rochester is able to change, to grow from the ashes, as it were. I like to think Thornfield burning cleansed him of his lies and passions, allowing him to accept Jane's love in a pure way."

Our discussion continues until our teacups are empty and our scones consumed. Much too soon, Harlow returns our dishes to the service tray. Her break is over. I want to ask her to join me for dinner so we can resume our discussion. However, I know where we would end up. Instead I ask, "Will you be working tomorrow, or are you going to work on your jewelry designs?"

She smiles shyly, "You always make it sound so high-class. I just string beads."

"You don't give yourself enough credit, Harlow. Your creations are lovely," I reprimand. Harlow does not take praise very well.

She shrugs, an American practice I abhor. "My mom made beautiful creations. I just string beads, and sometimes I luck out with an attractive combination and style."

"A lady graciously accepts all compliments," I impart,

taking on the task of teachable moments when they arise. There are many other things I'd like to teach her, but I don't feel she's ready.

She chortles, and I find the sound pleasant to my ears. "Well, that's the problem: I'm far from a lady. But, to answer your question, I asked for the day off, but I haven't decided what I'm going to do."

A day off? "And what are the options?" It's uncommon for her to take time away from work. If anything, she works as many shifts as the owner will give her.

"I'm not sure. It's been a long time since I've been to a movie; I may go into town and see that new sci-fi picture, or I might hike to Looking Glass Falls. I've heard it's beautiful, and I'd like to go before it gets too cold."

I nod, wishing I were going along. "I've wanted to go there too. Ms. Sheldon says in winter, the falls freeze vertically and reflect the sun like a mirror. I think I would choose that activity tomorrow. It should prove interesting to see the falls." I let my hopefulness for an invitation show on my face. I have far too much work, but spending a day with Harlow is something I'd truly like to do.

Her gaze leaves mine, and she pulls her plump bottom lip through her teeth before restlessly looking up. "Would, um… Would you like to… You can come if you want."

That invitation was ripped from her lips. The scrunched-up sour look on her face announces that she didn't invite me for any reason other than to be polite. But I'll take it. "I would like that. May I bring the picnic?" I ask.

She swallows, looking somewhat ill. "Sure, but none of that fancy English food."

I grin and nod. "I shall make sure of proper American fare."

She pauses by the floor-to-ceiling windows. "You have a remarkable view from here. I don't see how you get any work done."

"Do I? I never have time to sit around being unproductive by gazing out a window." My eyes follow through to the scene beyond. Yes. I've looked out the window many times, but I've never really taken the time to appreciate this sight.

"That's sad. You should make time." She blushes prettily and nervously rattles the dishes on the tray. "Well, I need to get back to the shop."

After she leaves, I followed her progress back to Tea Thyme then ring my assistant. "Ms. Sheldon, please step in." My gaze moves to the scene from my windows. It is a spectacular view. I've never really noticed.

In only a moment, Ms. Sheldon walks in my office, with her trusty pad and pen.

"Ms. Sheldon, please get me whatever one in America wears on a hike. Maybe a pair of trousers with all the pockets. You have record of my sizes. And would you contact my chef to prepare a suitable picnic?" I grin and add, "An American picnic."

Her eyes take on a decidedly cunning sparkle. "You're going on a picnic with Harlow?" she asks.

I busy myself with shuffling papers on my desk, "Yes," I say, not willing to add information.

There's a pause before she nods and says, "I'll get right on this."

As I'm straightening the folders, my eyes fall on the spot where the tea service had sat. In its place is a small sculpted dog figure. My mind goes back to the conversation I had with Harlow more than a month ago about my favored childhood pet. Monty was a chocolate and white cocker spaniel my Mum surprised me with on my tenth birthday. I believe I'd told Harlow about a memory I'd had of Monty scaling a rock wall when I'd fallen trying to climb up and shimmy down the other side. Monty ran home and brought the stablemaster back to rescue me. I'd broken my leg. After that, Mum never minded that Monty slept on my bed.

I smile and reach for the three-inch figure. It looks just like Monty. I set Monty down beside the other treasures that keep finding their way into my office. Some I'm sure she's made, and others I wonder if she rescued them from the trash bin. I chuckle as I look at the odd assortment. A tape dispenser in the shape of a frog. The tape looks like the frog's tongue sticking out. A pencil with a Big Ben eraser. A PEZ dispenser of Mr. Bean, an English actor that I had to research since I had no idea who Mr. Bean was. A snow globe of an English castle. Mostly silly childish trinkets, but they make me smile and give me a bit of a sentimental feeling of England.

After the first few had mysteriously shown up on my

desk, I'd confronted Harlow about leaving them, and she'd pretended to have no idea what I was talking about. Her mischievous eyes told me everything I needed to know about the secret gift giver.

My office phone buzzes. "Yes, Ms. Sheldon?"

"Mr. Maxwell is here for your meeting," Ms. Sheldon announces.

I take one final glance at Monty and smile. "Send him in, please."

CHAPTER FOUR

Harlow

I step on the elevator, balance the stupid silver tray on my hip, and punch the button quickly with a free finger. "You can come if you want," I mutter to myself and slap my head against the elevator wall. *Great, Low. Just great!* I've resisted all of his invitations, and now I go and blow it by asking him to go with me tomorrow.

Maybe I'll call his office and tell Ms. Sheldon to leave him a note that my plans have changed and I'm not going. But he'd looked so excited about going to Looking Glass Falls. I hate to let him down. Really, it will be no different from sitting in his office while he drinks his horrid tea. I'm not willing to admit that I'm beginning to enjoy the taste.

My relationship with Duke is a strange one. It's hard to believe that our unusual friendship developed over the lack of a proper cup of English tea. He still makes my heart flutter, and frankly, I'd read any stuffy old book and talk to him about it as long as I can sit and stare at him while we talk. Sometimes I catch him watching me, and I wonder… But then I laugh it off.

Kaylee looks up from the shelf of doughnuts she's restocking and grins. "How's Mr. Bigwig?"

I grin as I tie on my apron. "He's good," I answer then pick up the silver tray, carrying it to the back to take care of the dishes. Kaylee loves teasing me about Mr. Ainsworth—Duke. She thinks he has a crush on me. I wish.

"April was in here looking for you while you were gone. She wants you to call."

"Sure. I'll give her a call when I get off." I nod as I stack the teacups and saucers in the sink to wash. I take extra care with the delicate dishes; I know they must have been expensive.

"Go ahead and call her now. Baylee's here to help," Kaylee says.

"Okay. If you're sure." I wipe my hands on a mop rag and walk down the hall to the office. Kaylee has been such an incredible employer and friend. Leanne had her baby the week after I started working and decided to stay home with her new bundle of joy, so I've been working full-time since then. Sometimes I wonder if Kaylee figured out I'm homeless. Like giving me leftovers to take home and bringing me clothes she says she no longer likes. She's also never questioned the address I gave her on my application. I'd given her my Jersey address and said I wasn't sure of my new address at the time.

"Hey," Kaylee calls, and I turn back. "We need more tea charms. I sold the last one a few minutes ago."

My mouth drops open. I've made dozens of charms, and I can't believe how popular they've become. Kaylee charges five dollars for each charm, and she doesn't charge me a fee. Another thing I can't believe. With the money I've made, I've been able to order supplies and expand the designs. It's crazy! I shake my head and answer, "Okay. I'll bring you more tomorrow."

I dial April's number. She picks up on the first ring. "Hey, April. Kaylee said you wanted me to call?"

"Hey, girl! Yes, I did. She said you were with Duke. What's that about?"

I roll my eyes. I don't need another person thinking there's a romance brewing where there isn't one. Can't they see how ridiculous that even sounds? "Nothing. I just take him his afternoon tea. I think he misses his home."

"Just tea?" she teases.

I refuse to take the bait. I wonder if this is what it would be like to have sisters. As annoying as it is, I kinda like it. "Well, we talk about books and stuff. He's a really nice man."

"Harlow, you can't fool me. You like him!"

I have no idea how she got that out of what I said.

"Well, of course I do. I said he's nice. We sit and talk about books and drink tea and eat scones or biscuits, which are really cookies."

"I know we've not known each other for very long, but I know you well enough to hear what you aren't saying. We need to get together. How about I bring a pizza over tomorrow night and we can catch up, maybe watch a chick flick?"

A blaring horn blares in my head. "That sounds really good, but I've already got plans for tomorrow." I don't really, but I can't have her coming over to discover where I live.

"Oh, rats! Elias and I are leaving for California the next day for a few weeks, so let's plan on getting together when we get back."

I lean my head back against the office chair and give a relieved sigh. *Crisis averted.* "Sure. Definitely. Maybe Rachael and Kyle will be back from visiting his folks in Ireland, so we can invite Rachael as well."

"Sounds like a plan. Now, the reason I wanted to talk to you is because I have a huge favor to ask. I know this is last minute, so it's okay if you can't."

She sounds so cute when she's excited. I know, whatever it is, she can't wait to tell me. "April, what is it? You know I'll do it if I can. You and Rachael have been so wonderful to me."

"It's because we like you, and you're our friend.

Anyway, do you know the turquoise and coral necklace and earring set you made me?"

I chuckle. "I made it, so yes, I remember."

"Our producer saw mine and wants one. I told her it was an original but that I'd ask you about creating a piece for her." She squeals, and I have to jerk the phone from my ear to save my eardrums.

I rub my forehead. *No. No. No.* "Oh, April. You shouldn't have said that. I was just fooling around and thought they would look good with that denim dress you have."

"Harlow." Her voice takes on that don't-mess-with-me teacher tone. "You have got to get over your confidence issue. We've all told you how good your designs are. You could easily sell your pieces for big bucks. I mean, really, hasn't Ben wanted you to put some things in his art shop? He wouldn't have asked if he didn't think they would sell. And aren't your tea charms flying off the shelves faster than you can make them?"

Those don't count. "Ben was only being nice when you and Rachael put him on the spot. And I have no idea why the tea charms are selling so well. I'm sure their popularity won't last long."

April sighs loudly. "I give up. You're impossible. Harlow, you are very talented. Will you make Margorie a set or not?"

I guess I could. I'm already thinking of a design. Maybe it would be okay. "Sure, I will."

"Great. She asked if you'd use the same color combination, and I told her it would be at least two hundred and fifty dollars."

Two hundred and fifty dollars? The sum vibrates in my head like a church bell. "You did *what*?" I shout into the phone. "April! That's ridiculous!"

She giggles before quickly saying, "Listen, I've got to run. I'm getting a call on another line. I'll text Kaylee the address of where to mail them. I still don't understand why you don't have a cellphone."

Because I can't afford one. But April wouldn't know anything about that. After I end the call, I can't move from Kaylee's office chair. The thought of someone paying that much for something that I make is…unsettling. To think, if I sold five sets, I'd make more than I do in a month at Tea Thyme. I can't believe I'm even considering this. My mom would tell me not to count my chickens before they hatch.

When I walk back into the store, I see Baylee moving to the register to check a customer out. I remember what Kaylee said about keeping Baylee from checking out, so I quickly cut her off. "Hey, Baylee. I can check Ms. Brown out, so you can go ahead and take your break."

After I ring the sale and wish Ms. Brown a good day, I turn to find Baylee hasn't left. She looks upset and a tad angry, an emotion I've never seen from her. I honestly didn't know she was capable. "Bay, are you okay?"

Baylee looks me straight in the eyes and asks, "She told you not to let me ring up customers, didn't she?"

I don't even pretend I don't know who she's talking about. I answer her honestly. "She did."

Baylee's whole body take on a disappointed look. She lowers her head and nods several times. "I can do it myself. I don't need help. There was only one time I got mixed up, and that was because it was a new register. I've learned this one, and I can do it."

Her head tips up, and our eyes meet. This is important to her. "Okay," I agree.

"So, you'll let me?" she asks softly.

I nod and smile. "If you say you can do it, that's fine with me."

The sunny smile I've grown to love reappears on her face. "Okay. Good. If I need help, I'll ask."

I watch Baylee get back to work wiping the counter down as if she'd not been upset only a few moments ago. I have no idea what just happened, but I do know determination when I see it, and Baylee Conrad is one determined woman.

By the end of my shift, I still hadn't left a message canceling with Duke. I know it's dangerous to allow myself to get closer to him. Not only because I've been silently pining for the owner of the apartment complex, but also because I've been living in that complex illegally since Dad left me stranded. I would like to think that Duke wouldn't have me arrested if he found out, but I don't want to take the chance.

The town of Treemont is a slow-moving Southern town

I've come to love. I have friends, and for the first time in my life, I feel like I belong someplace.

I don't like lying to everyone about being homeless, but soon I'll actually be able to rent my own apartment. I've already saved a nice nest egg thanks to my tea charms. I can't afford White Oaks, but there are some clean duplex apartments across town.

Once I've visited the apartment gym to bathe, I make my way back up the stairs to my room. I hang up my borrowed wet towel and pull on a t-shirt to sleep in. I really feel bad for sneaking into the gym to shower, but there's no way I'm going without a shower. I am courteous by using only one towel each week. Somehow that makes it better in my mind.

I hang the Tea Thyme shirt and black uniform pants I'd been wearing from hooks I'd placed on the shelves I'd made from an old pallet I'd found in the alley behind the store. It's crazy how many things show up at the trash bins. I found a perfectly good area rug that now covers my floor, a lawn chair, and I even rescued a desk that was missing a leg. I MacGyvered a leg from some of the pallet wood, and now, with my pretty lamp, I have an excellent place to work on my jewelry. My little home is becoming very comfortable.

Turning the lamp off, I climb into my makeshift bed and stare at the ceiling. I like this life I've made. My last conscious thought is about Duke and Looking Glass Falls and...dreaming of his lips on mine.

The next morning, just as I'm stepping off the elevator on Duke's office floor, I hear behind me a very distinctive British accent saying, "Good morning, Harlow."

I whirl around in time to see...Duke? "Morning, Mr.—I mean, Duke." It is him. I've never seen him dressed in anything other than a suit. The black, long-sleeved t-shirt fits his chest and arms like a second skin. I never imagined he was so...developed. My eyes go directly to his biceps, and I may have whined just a little. Were I to wrap both my hands, finger-to-finger, around those taut muscles, I don't think they would meet. I want to touch them and see if they're as hard as they appear. The span of his chest is wide, with rippling abs that dip to a trim waist. I decide I love that tight black shirt.

"I would have fetched you from your apartment, but I didn't know your number." He waits patiently for me to provide my address.

My appreciation of his stellar body is suddenly consumed by anxiety. Instead of answering, I turn toward the elevator I'd just gotten off, saying, "I guess we better go. You know, get an early start and all. We could drive right up to the falls, but I thought hiking to them would be more fun. Kaylee said we could Uber close, then there's a walking path through the woods we can take."

Duke follows me into the elevator. "Uber?" he asks. "Is that like a taxi?" he asks with distaste.

A small grin plays at the corner of my lips. "Yeah."

"We'll take my car," he says, raising his phone to his ear as we watch the floor numbers go by, the subject obviously settled. He's certainly used to getting his way.

By the time we get downstairs, a big black limousine and driver are waiting for us. I can't help it; I start to giggle.

He pauses and turns to me with questioning eyes. "Is there some issue with taking my car?"

I bite my lips to stop the giggles and shake my head. "No. I just thought you meant we could take your car. You know, like…" Suddenly, I realize there isn't any way I can explain why I find it funny. Which only makes me chuckle again. To someone like Duke, a car and driver isn't out of the ordinary. "Never mind. Let's go." Just like he did in the elevator, I dismiss the subject.

Duke hands the driver a large wooden basket I hadn't even noticed. He really packed for a picnic. A sandwich, a bag of chips, and a bottle of water stuffed in my backpack is what I would have had if I'd been by myself. I shrug and open the car door, sliding into the softest leather seats. I want to moan from the luxurious feeling cuddling my body. When Duke doesn't join me, I bend over and peer out the door to find Duke and his driver with the most startled looks on their faces. "Is something wrong?" I ask. Both men shake their heads in unison. When Duke slides in beside me and waits for his driver to shut the door I realize my blunder. "I guess I wasn't supposed to get in myself, huh?"

"Jeffrey was a bit put out, but I think he'll recover," he says, with an amused sparkle in his eyes.

Duke's lifestyle is so foreign to me, and not just because he's English and speaks with a dreamy accent. I tip my head wondering what he sounds like during sex. The suddenly sensitive tips of my nipples brush against my t-shirt. No, in the throes of passion would sound more apropos. Apropos? Oh, lordy. Now he has me sounding all proper. Besides, I don't need to have thoughts of sex and Duke at the same time. "Do you ever drive?" I ask, to get my brain switched to a safe subject.

He gives me a curious look, almost like he'd been privy to my secret thought, then glances out the window as we pull out of the parking lot. "I do sometimes, when I'm home in England."

When he's gone for a week or two, I have wondered where he goes. Not that I've noticed, that is. "I thought you lived here, on the top floor of your office building."

He nods and turns my way. "I do. Well, as often as I can. I'm afraid duty calls me home much too often."

I can certainly understand about duty. "But you prefer to live here?"

He seems deep in thought for a moment before he answers. "I love England, but I find I like who I am here better," he admits.

That's a revealing and curious thing to say. "What's the difference?"

He turns and smiles at me. "One is a lot happier, for one

thing. In America, I follow my own pursuits. I have many responsibilities back home. My father passed a few years ago, and now I must look after his holdings and take care of my mother."

I wonder if he feels burdened by that responsibility. I somehow think not. "I'm sorry for your loss. Looking after your mom…that's a very sweet thing to do. I bet you she misses you."

He nods and smiles. "She does. We talk almost every day. Mostly, my mum talks, and I listen."

My mom had always said to look for a man who treats his mother well. "Ah, that makes it even sweeter. When are you going home again?"

His smile fades. "Sooner than I'd planned. My cousin is getting married soon, and I must attend."

I change the topic. I want his smile back. "Do you know I've come into your office for months now, and I have no idea what you do? I mean, I know you own White Oaks, but you're always busy when I come to tea. Are you really just playing Candy Crush on your computer?" He laughs, and my wayward heart flutters. He's loosened up so much since I first met him. I'd like to think I have a small part in that transformation.

"Someday you must tell me what this Candy Crush is. I can assure you I am working. I have interests in many things. I suppose you'd call me an entrepreneur. Like re-designing the old mill into green-living apartments then turning the entire complex into a community of sorts."

I knew he was extremely smart and the mastermind behind White Oaks. "It's really remarkable what you've done."

"Thank you. I'm very proud of what my team has accomplished with this project. I feel it's everyone's responsibility to leave the smallest carbon footprint possible. It is my hope that others will see our community here and follow suit."

Such a commendable goal. I've only heard good things said about Duke and the way he manages White Oaks since working at Tea Thyme. That says a lot about a man. "So, you have more businesses like this?"

"Yes. I have a development department that seeks out interesting projects that focus on improving the environment. Where are you from originally?" He quickly flips the subject to me.

I get the message. He doesn't like to talk about himself. I don't either, so what are we going to do for the rest of the afternoon? The inquisition has begun. "Up north, in New Jersey," I answer vaguely.

"And why did you move to North Carolina?"

I pause and sigh. I don't like lying. "Just, um, needed a change of scenery. My dad and I were traveling and found this town."

He nodded knowingly. "So, you live with your dad?"

The car starts to bounce. "No, he, um, continued his travels, and I decided to stay." I look out the window and notice we've turned down a dirt road. After less than a mile, his driver comes to a stop.

Duke looks around me with a grin and says, "I suppose this is where we begin our hike."

"Yes, Kaylee said to go that way"—I point out the left window—"and we'll eventually hear the falls." Jeffrey opens Duke's door, and we both slide out. "Aren't you forgetting the picnic basket?" I mean, I'm all about the food. Especially if I don't have to buy it.

"Jeffrey will use the faster route by driving to the falls, and he will have it waiting for us when we arrive," he explains.

Well, that's convenient. Heaven forbid we have to carry a food hamper. "Oh, okay. That sounds good." What it must be like to have someone on standby to make your life easier…

"What's that look for?" he pauses and asks.

I shrug my backpack onto my shoulders before saying, "Nothing."

Duke crosses his arms over his chest, and my eyes are pulled back to that impressive area. "Harlow, we're not going to have a pleasant day if you don't answer my questions."

I watch his limousine disappear down the dirt road. "I was just trying to imagine what it would be like to have people like Jeffrey and Ms. Sheldon." I duck into the trees and start walking toward the falls. Duke follows beside me.

"It's their job, Harlow. They are compensated for their work," he explains.

We come to a fallen log, and Duke takes my hand to help me over. At first, I'm startled by his touch and then by his thoughtfulness. Such a simple, polite gesture makes me feel... "Do you have a housekeeper, too?" I ask, to cover my inability to own that emotion.

"I have several household staff."

As soon as I'm across the log, he releases my hand. And I miss his touch. "Like what?"

"Ms. Bennett oversees the household. A chef prepares my meals, and I believe there are several housekeepers. Oh, and Edward, my valet. However, Edward will be going back to England soon. His daughter just presented him with his first grandson."

I stop in my tracks and meet his gaze. He's serious. Do people really have those anymore? "Valet? You mean someone who dresses you?"

He looks insulted by my question. "Among other things."

I chuckle and I want to laugh so bad. "Are you serious? You can't dress yourself?"

If possible, he straightens his six-foot-whatever frame even more, peers down his chiseled nose, and replies, "I can assure you I have no problems with buttons and zips."

I can't even comprehend his level of wealth. "Have you always been rich?"

His chin tips and his lips thin. "I forget how straightfor-ward you Americans are."

No generalization there, but he's right. That is rude to ask. "I'm sorry. I shouldn't have asked that." We start walking again, and I can hear the distant roar of the falls as we get closer.

"It's fine. Yes, my family have always been well off. I suppose it is different to someone..." He stumbles, his impeccable manners not allowing him to complete his observation.

"Hey, it's okay. I'm not embarrassed by my life. Before I moved here, I worked as a receptionist at a dentist's office, kept the books for a garage, and cleaned several offices after hours. I'm not a stranger to getting by or working paycheck to paycheck." *I'm just embarrassed about living in your building illegally.*

His brows raise. "Three jobs. That seems quite exces-sive. So, you studied accounting in school?"

I shake my head and pull a leaf from a passing tree. "No, I just picked it up on my own. Luckily, Eddie, my boss, didn't mind a few slips at first, before I got the hang of it."

"That is quite a feat. I knew you were a smart woman from our book discussions. What did you study in school?"

I toss the leaf away and sigh. "I...didn't go to college." Still a sore point for me.

We walk in silence for a few moments before he offers, "College isn't for everyone."

"I guess. I would have liked to have gone; it just wasn't possible. My mom was killed in a car accident, and my dad was never the same. He couldn't work, so I took care of him."

He stopped walking and turned to me. "How old were you, Harlow?"

I adjust my backpack and answer, "Sixteen." Our eyes meet, and I can almost feel his understanding and compassion. I clear my throat at the sudden weird feeling between us and start walking. The falls can't be much farther.

He touches my arm to get my attention, and my skin sizzles under his light touch. "I'm sorry about your mum, and I'm sorry you had to go through that. But your dad must be better now, since he's traveling."

As I'm trying to come up with an answer, we break through the trees. "Oh look, there are the falls!" I call out as I run ahead to get closer. The sight before our eyes is spectacular. The falls rise at least thirty feet above us and drop into a pond at the base, in a white, frothy foam which flows into a fast-moving river.

We stand on a grassy bank a few feet from the river, both lost in our appreciation of the sight before us. "I don't think I've ever seen anything more beautiful," I say in wonder.

"I have," Duke says quietly.

I turn my head, and our eyes met. He hadn't been looking at the falls. My heart starts to flutter. I've never had someone look at me so intensely or make me feel like a desirable woman. "What?" I asked, just to clarify.

He nods toward the falls. "In England, we have beautiful waterfalls as well."

I feel my face warm. *Of course. I'm such an idiot.* "Oh, right." I look down, hoping the ground will open up so I could fall in. I catch a glimpse of something fluttering behind us. "Would you look at that? Who does something so…" I was at a loss for words as I point to a shady spot underneath a tree, where a dining table and chairs has been set up.

"Civilized?" Duke offers. "I believe that would be our picnic."

"Our picnic?" I ask and start walking toward the elegantly dressed table with a linen tablecloth, real china dishes, and even a vase of mixed wildflowers. "Is this the way you have picnics in England?" I turn to Duke with my eyes probably as big as saucers. "This is incredible," I have to admit.

Duke laughs, and I startle. My insides go to mush. That's the first time I've ever heard him laugh. A glance at his face has my stomach doing flips.

"I will admit that Jeffrey and Ms. Sheldon may have gone a bit overboard."

He looks so relaxed. It's a good look on him. "I'm almost afraid to ask what's under the domed lids."

"I asked for a traditional American picnic. Shall we find out what we have?" He picks up the lid from my plate.

I start laughing. "This is perfect!" Fried chicken, potato salad, deviled eggs and some type of pasta salad. Duke lifts another lid and we find a crystal bowl of fresh sliced fruit—watermelon, grapes, strawberries and blueberries. I shake my head in disbelief. "This is amazing, Duke."

He smiles, and his face softens. "I'm glad you approve. Shall we?"

"Most definitely," I say, but my attention is drawn to his hands when he picks up his knife and fork to cut a piece of chicken. "Hang on there." I pick up a chicken leg. "If you're on an American picnic, this is how we do it in the States." I take a bite out of the juicy meat, closing my eyes to enjoy the delicious flavor. I've not had a meal like this in so long. I think I may pass out just from the smell. When I open my eyes, Duke is fixated on my mouth. "Oh, do I have something on my face?" I ask, swiping my linen napkin across my lips. "There, did I get it?" I ask.

Duke clears his throat. "Um, yes. Perfect," he says as he picks up a chicken leg.

He holds the meat with his fingers, but his little finger is ever so properly raised. I smother my laughter behind my napkin. "So, admit it, you've never been on a picnic, have you?"

He chews and swallows before answering. "I most certainly have. When I was a lad, my parents would often have a picnic by a pond in our backyard. We'd stay most of the afternoon. Just lounging around, taking a walk, playing games, or just reading."

"That sounds like a wonderful memory." The thoughts make him seem happy.

His fork pauses in the air, and I can tell in his mind he's someplace else. He shakes his head to clear whatever image he'd painted. "It was a wonderful place to grow up. My mum still lives there."

"Were you close with your father?" I ask.

"Yes. Well, as much as we could be, given our circumstances. My father was a remarkable man, but he didn't see the importance of reevaluating what we put out in the world," he says, a note of irritation in his voice.

A gentle breeze flutters the tablecloth. "How long had they been married?"

"Thirty-eight years. What about your parents?" Duke asks.

"My mom and dad met in school. My dad says that Mom was the only reason he passed his English classes. They'd been married twenty-seven years when my mom was hit by a bus and killed."

Our gazes meet over the top of the beautiful flowers decorating the center of the table. "My condolences."

Sadly, I nod. "Thank you."

"Is that why he's traveling?" Duke asks.

"Yes." I take another bite of the delicious potato salad, hoping Duke will change the subject. Luckily, we finish lunch without any other questions I don't want to answer.

"Shall we walk down to the water's edge?" Duke suggests as we both push back from the table.

He offers his hand to help me up. I do give a bit of thought to my reaction to his touch, but I place my hand in his anyway. "That sounds lovely."

"I've heard the Groundling is playing at the Asheville Theater. Have you been?" Duke asks as we near the water's edge.

I'm wondering if he realizes he's still holding my hand or if he forgot. I don't care as long as he doesn't let go. "No. I'm afraid I've never been to live theater. I think the last movie I saw was Avatar in the movie theater."

His brows pull together as he tries to place the movie. "I don't believe I've seen that one."

There's never been a more clear-cut division of class. I thought everyone had seen Avatar. Then again, I can't imagine the blue people holding any appeal to the Ainsworth family.

He looks apprehensive as he says, "I can get tickets. Would you like to attend with me this Saturday?" he asks.

He's invited me to things before, but I've always said no. First because I had nothing to wear, and second because, well, get real. Why would Duke ask me out? I think he's only asked to be polite. "Oh." I pause and look down at the grass and worry my bottom lip between my teeth as I try to come up with a reason to decline. Then I look up, and our gazes meet. His eyes are on my lips, and I feel them move to my eyes, where he captures my breath. I have a sense we're connecting on a whole other level. My silly heart flutters to life when he leans forward with his eyes going straight to my lips. I lean into him and...

What happens next isn't really clear in my mind. Somehow, I find myself falling backward, my arms and legs flailing, and a terrified screech leaves my mouth as I fly through the air. In the corner of my eyes I see Duke's outstretched hands, and I make a last attempt to grab on. But I can't, and I'm falling—

"Harlow!" Duke calls out frantically just before frigid water closes around me and pulls me down. The strong current from the falls carries me downriver quickly as I fight to break free. An iron band clamps on my arm, and I know without a doubt it's Duke. I break through the surface and immediately wrap my arms and legs around his body as I fight to cough water from my lungs. His arms wrap tightly around me, holding me, keeping me safe. "Are you all right?" he asks and tightens his grip.

I nod, unable to speak, and it has nothing to do with the water I ingested. I look up at Duke; his pupils dilate and move down to my lips. My insides clench. I grip him tighter with my legs in the waist-deep water and feel the unmistakable evidence of his arousal. My lashes flutter to fix on his strong, seductive lips. I know it's going to happen. I'm frozen as he leans closer, and my breath catches.

"Harlow?" he asks, his voice thick from the adrenalin rush.

I watch his lips as they move, asking for what we both want. "Yes," I whisper, and his lips slowly lower and gently land on mine. The cold temperature of the early fall water does nothing to cool the burning desire raging through my veins. Duke pulls me closer to his hard body as my hands tighten around his neck, pressing my breasts into his chest. His lips leave mine. I whimper until they land on my neck, then my teeth begin to chatter.

The sound of my frigid state shocks us both into action like a literal cold-water bath. I drop to my feet and Duke keeps a hand on my arm to keep me from being sucked into the current again. Our chests heave as water drips down our bodies; our eyes connect, and regret washes over me. Regret that I kissed Duke, or regret that it ended much too soon? I'm not certain.

Duke's breathing is wild and erratic. "I'm sorry, Harlow. While I am not sorry about that kiss, I should have considered your comfort."

"I was very comfortable," I say, then realize how silly that sounded.

He grins and runs his thumb over my bottom lip. "Your lips are turning blue. Come, let's get you home and into some dry clothes." Jeffrey was waiting for us in the parking lot with the car running and a blanket in his hands. Duke wraps the blanket around me and then tucks me into his side to warm me up. I have absolutely no problem with this.

On the ride back to White Oaks, neither one of us mentions what happened in the river. I'm still trying to wrap my head around it all, and how could one simple kiss have affected me so strongly. I decide I don't care because I'm the happiest I've been in...years.

"Duke." I look up into his eyes and smile. "Even with our unscheduled bath, this was the best day ever." I bite my lip and anxiously look down at my fidgeting hands.

"For me, too." He closes his warm hands over my chilled ones.

I shiver as his touch flushes through my body, taking away most of the cold. "Thank you for spending my birthday with me." My happiness is evident by the wide smile and chattering teeth decorating my face.

His brows raise and he asks, "It's your birthday? Why didn't you tell me?"

I shrug and turn to look out the window. "It doesn't matter. I got what I want." *Boy, did I.* I've dreamed about kissing Duke since the day I met him. The real thing was so much better. I sneak peeks during the drive, and I don't understand why he looks upset at not knowing about my birthday.

When we get back to White Oaks, Jeffrey opens the car door, and Duke gets out first, taking my hand to help me. I unwrap myself from the blanket and hand it back.

"Are you sure I can't walk you up?" Duke asks.

"I'm sure. Thanks again." I stretch up on my toes and kiss his cheek. *Best birthday ever*, I think as I run inside.

Just as I'm pushing the button to go up, a hand pops through the opening. "Excuse me, dear." Ms. Edna pokes her head in and smiles. "We've been watching for you to come home."

I go ahead and step out of the elevator, as I know the apartment matriarchs won't be quick with whatever they have to say. I did have dinner with them one night, and I've never laughed so much. I can only imagine what they were like in their younger days. They filled me so full I had to waddle home with the containers of leftovers they insisted I take. Even though I had no way to keep things cold, I ate as much as I could the next morning, and then I took the rest for my lunch and kept it in the cooler at work. That's one problem I haven't found a solution for in my "apartment."

"Hi, Ms. Edna. Ms. Blanche. How are you ladies today?" Kaylee thinks they must be in their seventies, but nobody is brave enough to ask. If you judge by their energy level, then I'd say fifties.

"Oh, we're fine, dear. You look a bit damp, though," Ms. Edna says with a grin.

Ms. Blanche adds, "Your young man did, too."

"My young man? Do you mean Duke?" I ask then shake my head quickly in denial. "Oh, he's not—"

Ms. Blanche interrupts, patting my soggy sleeve, "Now don't try to deny it, dear. Mr. Ainsworth has never once taken off work in the middle of the day in the ten years we've known him."

Ms. Edna bites her lips and grins, "Especially not to go on a picnic."

This is not going well. My teeth start to chatter again. I wrap my arms around myself and remind them, "You said you were looking for me? Is there something I can do for you?"

"Oh, no, dear. We just wanted to give you this." Ms. Blanche nudges Ms. Edna, who produces a round plastic cake holder from a brown paper shopping bag.

I take it from her. "What's this for?" My eyes pinch together.

Ms. Edna smiles and says, "Why, for your birthday, silly."

Ms. Blanche clasps her hands together. "We couldn't let the day end without giving you your cake."

"We made it especially for you," Ms. Edna says. Then, lowering her voice to a whisper, she adds, "Each layer is soaked in a bit of our fruit punch." Then she squinches her nose up in delight.

I chuckle, because I've heard about their famous fruit punch, and I've been warned to stay away from the lethal drink. But I am speechless that they know it's my birthday and that they would take the time to make me a cake. I really don't know what to say. My eyes start to sting. "Thank you. That was very sweet of you. I can't even remember the last time I had a birthday cake."

"Well, we won't let that happen again." Ms. Blanche says and gives me an awkward, wet hug, trying not to get her neon-green-and-pink track suit wet.

Ms. Edna follows by leaning in and giving me a kiss on

my cheek. "Now you go on up and get dried off. Happy birthday, dear."

This time when I get back on the elevator, my teeth are chattering and my hands are shivering so badly I have to grip the cake so I don't drop it, but I have a smile on my face and maybe a tear in my eye. I've never felt so much a part of a community. And I'm lying to them all. I sneeze as I push the button for the third floor.

CHAPTER FIVE

Duke

After making a stop at my penthouse to change into dry clothes, I ride down to my office and all the work I have yet to do. Today's outing with Harlow was nothing like I had anticipated. I certainly never expected that kiss. Without a doubt, I'll be spending sleepless hours reliving the feel of her sweet lips on mine. And then her shy admission that today is her birthday. Had I known, I would have done something a bit more special than trampling through the woods for a picnic. *No.* I run my hand along my chin and grin as the elevator doors open. Today was perfect. I pause on the way into my office and ask, "Ms. Sheldon. Would you please send Harlow flowers?"

She purses her lips as she makes note of my request, but not before I see the slight upward curve of a threatening grin. "Certainly. What would you like?" she says with complete professionalism.

I pause to consider my options. Roses don't seem like Harlow, nor do any of the other boutique flowers I've sent to countless women over the years. "Something bright and colorful. Today's her birthday. Maybe daisies, sunflowers, and violets." That sounds like a happy arrangement.

She looks up, and her eyes warm. "I didn't know today was Harlow's birthday. I would have baked her a cake." She fingers a lovely blue-and-gold necklace. "She's such a sweet girl. Did you know she made this beautiful necklace for me? One day I commented that my granddaughter would like a necklace she was wearing, and she took it off and gave it to me. Then, a few weeks later, she gave me this and said it would match my blue suit. And she wouldn't take money for either one."

I've never known anyone like Harlow. The more I find out about her, the more fascinating she becomes. "It's quite lovely."

"Is there anything else, sir?" Ms. Sheldon asks.

I shake my head and push off to get some work done. I'm already behind. "Look her apartment number up in the resident database and have them delivered today," I call over my shoulder.

I'm back at my desk, ready to make up for the three hours I spent today with Harlow. I've never taken such a long lunch break, but I guess that doesn't really matter. I would do it all over again just for the few minutes I held her in my arms and kissed her lips. I've never lost myself in a kiss before. Had the sound of her chattering teeth not connected with my brain, I'm afraid I would have taken her right there in the middle of the river.

I push those thoughts aside and dive back into my work. It's after five when Ms. Sheldon knocks on my office door. She steps in with a confused look on her face. A look I'm not used to seeing on her. She's always been competent and efficient.

"I'm sorry, sir. I can't locate Harlow's apartment number. She's not in the database."

That's impossible. She has to be. "Maybe she's under a different name."

She shakes her head slowly. "That's what I assumed as well. I contacted Kaylee over at Tea Thyme and she doesn't know her apartment number, either."

I tap my pencil on my desk and suggest, "Have Kaylee give you her phone number and call her."

Again, she shakes her head. "Another dead end, I'm afraid. Harlow doesn't have a phone."

My eyes narrow. Doesn't have a phone? Is that even possible? "No phone?" I repeat to make sure I understood her correctly.

Her hands splay upward, "No, sir."

How could my managers have been so negligent in entering her data? Before today, I would have thought that impossible. "She moved here in April or May of this year. Search all the contracts for that time."

"I did sir. And I contacted each one. There is no Harlow Davidson in the books."

Obviously, management has made a huge mistake. I'll need to make a note to meet with them immediately. "Take the flowers over to Tea Thyme, and she can get them when she goes to work tomorrow. I'll get this straightened out when she brings my tea."

Long after Ms. Sheldon leaves my office, I'm left pondering what could have happened to cause a paperless trail to Harlow. My eyes land on the frog tape dispenser, and it makes me smile. Maybe she's subletting—even though that's not allowed. Or she could be house-sitting for someone who's out of the country for an extended period of time. I dismiss the issue and get back to work. There could be many reasons why Ms. Sheldon couldn't find her.

However, the next day when Harlow brings my tea, none of the questions I wanted to ask her seem important, because as soon as she walks in my office, I know something is wrong. Her skin is pale, her nose a bright red, and she's flushed in the face like she's running a temperature.

"Harlow, you're sick." I rush around my desk to get to her.

"No. I'm fine. Thank you for the flowers. They were beautiful." She manages a weak smile.

I take the tray from her before she drops it and set it on

my desk. She slumps into a chair. I touch her forehead, and it's as I suspected; she's burning up.

"You need to see a doctor," I say, reaching for a box of tissues to pull a few out.

Harlow grabs them just in time for her sneeze. "No. I'm fine. It's just a little cold. I'll be good as new tomorrow. I've got to work," she says in a husky voice.

I roll my eyes, an expression I can't believe I've adopted, but it feels warranted. I pick up my office phone and push a few buttons. "Good day, Kaylee. Harlow is going to take the afternoon off. She is unwell."

"Good. I've been trying all morning to get her to go home," Kaylee says.

"I'll see that she does," I assure her, before I hung up and turn to Harlow, ready for a fight. I grin when I find she's fallen asleep in my chair.

I step quietly to the door, "Ms. Sheldon, would you call Dr. Henson and ask him to stop by? Harlow isn't feeling well."

I carry Harlow to the leather couch and cover her shivering body with a blanket. However, I'm unable to concentrate on my work with her only a few feet from me. I can't keep myself from just watching her sleep. Less than an hour later, Ms. Sheldon ushers in Dr. Henson. Harlow hasn't moved in all that time.

An irritated woman wakes while her blood pressure is being taken. Her bloodshot eyes try to intimidate me, but she misses the mark. A cute red nose doesn't help, either. "I called for the doctor. You're sick," I tell her, grinning as she fights a sneeze.

Finally defeated, she turns her head and sneezes into her elbow. Twice. "It's just a cold. I don't need a doctor," she says, a few octaves lower than normal.

Dr. Henson puts his blood pressure cuff away and gets out a thermometer. "Let me be the judge of that, young lady. Open."

Harlow glares at me the entire time the thermometer is in her mouth.

When the chirp sounds, Dr. Henson's brow furrows. "That's a very high temperature you have there." He puts the instrument away and feels the glands on her neck. Nodding, he says, "Plus, your glands are swollen."

I blame myself for this. I should have insisted she dry off quicker. "We both took a dip in the river yesterday, by accident, I can assure you."

"Well, that alone wouldn't have been the cause in and of itself. However, prolonged exposure to cold or chill could have been a contributing factor," Doctor Henson clarifies as he packs his medical bag.

"Thank you for coming, Doctor, but it was totally unnecessary," Harlow croaks and sneezes three times in a row.

"Well, it's that time of the year. Cold and flu season, I'm afraid. Over the counter Tylenol will help with the fever. Drink lots of fluids, and I'll check back tomorrow. If she's not doing better, a round of antibiotics may be in order."

Doctor Henson picks up his bag, and we both watch him leave. A movement in the corner of my eye sends me rushing forward. "Where do you think you're going?"

"Home." Her voice is now barely a whisper.

She struggles to stand up. I push her back down and get a piercing look because of my helpfulness. "You are as weak as a kitten. Frankly, I'm surprised you could get out of bed this morning. You should have called in sick."

"I don't need help," she says, pushing to her feet, swaying, and then falling into my arms. I scoop her up and head to the elevator. We ride it down in silence. I walk into the apartment building and head to the elevator, and she begins to struggle in my arms.

"Put me down. I can get there from here," she insists and almost jumps from my arms.

"Harlow, stop. I'm taking you to your door. If you don't want me to come in, fine. But I'm at least taking you that far." I move to pick her back up, but she side-steps away from me and holds a bracing hand in front of her. I want to help her, but I stop so she'll slow down.

She shakes her head and uses the wall for support as she walks away from me. "No, you're not. Duke, I've got it. Thank you for seeing me home, but I can take it from here."

She's in the elevator, and the doors are closing before I can jump on. She's the most stubborn woman I've ever met. Why can't she listen to reason? I watch the floor numbers and can't understand why they stopped at the third floor. I wait, thinking she hit the wrong number by accident, but the car doesn't move. I scratch my chin. I've not yet begun renovations on that floor, so why would Harlow get off there?

I push the button to recall the elevator. When I get off at the third floor, the cold air hits my face, which is to be expected since there's no heating or air installed. Everything is just as I remembered. The floor is ready for reconstruction. I hear a sneeze. My brows pull together as I head toward the sound. This makes no sense. Why would Harlow be up here?

As I near the end of the building, it appears the workmen left the walls standing to form a room. Usually this would be a place to store their tools while working on the floor. Another sneeze coming from inside the room makes me pause and quietly approach the open door.

I peer around the corner and can't believe what I've found. Evidently, Harlow's apartment. My eyes see red at the sight of her curled up on a bed of blankets, shivering. She's been living here. This…this is her home. No wonder she's sick. She spent the night cold and wet. I have no idea what's going on, but it stops now.

I try to keep my voice from sounding as angry as I am. "Harlow. What are you doing in here?"

She turns her head but doesn't raise it. "Duke, I really don't feel well. I just want to go to sleep. You can yell at me tomorrow." Her eyes close, and her breathing is labored.

I bend to pick her up. This isn't the time for answers. Harlow needs help, and she's going to get it.

"Duke, what are you doing?" she asks weakly and tries to struggle in my arms, but she doesn't have any energy.

I hold her close. "You are coming home with me," I gently tell her.

Her eyes pop open. "What? No!"

I raise my chin and stare into her droopy eyes. "You don't have a choice. You can come home with me and let me take care of you, or I can call the police and report your illegal residence." I wait for her next argument. It's not going to work. She's stubborn, but so am I. Especially when her health is concerned.

Her body finally relaxes into mine, and she surrenders. "Fine. I'll go with you. But I can walk."

I don't even wait for that argument. "No, you can't." I take her to my penthouse and tuck her into bed, feed her two Tylenol, and stand by the bed while she drinks an entire bottle of water. She's asleep before I close her bedroom door.

I stop in and ask Ms. Bennett to keep an eye on Harlow. Then I grab a suitcase from my closet and go back to the third floor. Standing in the middle of the small room, I can't believe she's been living here. All these months and she's been living like this. I carefully replace boxes of beads and tools into the yellow plastic box and then clear the room of all her things. It doesn't take long. She has pitifully few possessions. Again, I ask myself: Why? I look around the now-empty room and consider my options. I don't want her to have any way to return. I'll have the construction crew nail up the floor from the elevator if I have to.

I carry everything back to my home and call Ms. Sheldon to let her know I'm taking the rest of the day off. She sounds surprised, but really no more so than I am. For the rest of the day and night, I take care of Harlow.

In the middle of the night, her fever spikes, and her shivering becomes uncontrollable. Even with extra blankets, she's still shaking. I kick off my shoes and crawl into bed and tuck her body against mine. In only a few moments, she's calmed and resting peacefully. Eventually, I fall asleep with her in my arms. I've never felt so at peace.

CHAPTER SIX

Harlow

The smell of bacon tickles my senses as I work to open my sandpaper-filled eyes. I blink and then blink again because I still have no idea where I am. Neither the king-size bed nor the beautiful bedroom is familiar to me. I would have remembered. I raise the softest white comforter I've ever felt and peek underneath. I'm wearing my t-shirt and panties, but no bra and no pants. How…

The bedroom door opens. I jump, grabbing the blanket to my chin. Duke walks through the door with a tray in his hands, and my breath catches in my throat. His eyes stay on my face. I want to crawl under the fluffy blanket because I have a feeling I know who removed my pants and bra. I feel myself blush, and this time it's not from fever.

"Well, good morning. You are looking better today," he says, placing the tray on a side table.

"Where am I?" I ask, following him with my eyes around the room.

He disappears behind a door. I hear water running for a moment before he comes back in the bedroom, carrying a wet hand towel, which he gives to me. "You don't remember?"

I pause to think as I clean my hands with the warm towel. "I brought your tea to your office. Was it yesterday?"

He adjusts a few pillows behind my back. "That's right. But that was two days ago, then you fell asleep on my couch."

I've been out of it for two days? I must have been sicker than I thought. "There was a doctor."

"Yes, Dr. Henson. He'll be stopping by later today. He came yesterday, gave you an antibiotic shot, and left some medication for you. Ms. Bennett and I have been taking care of you."

That's when I remember something I wish I could block out. In my mind I re-run the image of Duke finding me on the third floor and the anger on his face. Suddenly, I feel exhausted. "Um. I can explain about—"

"And I expect you to, but later. When you're feeling better. Right now, let me carry you to the bathroom, and then you can try some eggs and toast for breakfast," he says, with much more understanding than I deserve.

I throw the cover back and swing my legs over the side. There's no way he's carrying me into the bathroom. How embarrassing. "I can get there on my own." I push to my feet, and the room begins to spin.

I sway and would have gone down if Duke hadn't scooped me up in his arms. "Why can't you for once listen? You are the most stubborn woman I've ever met."

I rest my head on his chest and just breath in his delicious scent.

"I thought you might want to change clothes. I hope what I left for you meets with your approval." Gently he sits me down in the bathroom and closes the door on his way out. My gosh! The bathroom is incredible! My eyes linger on the tub that's big enough for two. I'd love a soak, but I'd probably fall asleep. I want to take a shower, but I'm afraid I can't stand up long enough, and I certainly don't want Duke to have to carry my naked butt back to bed.

I use the toothbrush Duke had so thoughtfully laid out for me, wash my face, and change into a pair of blue silk lounge pants and a white tank top. I've never worn anything so fine. They fit perfectly, and my imagination runs away with thoughts of who they belong to. I'm not going to think too hard on that, because these are the most sinfully comfortable clothes I've ever worn. Suddenly, I'm exhausted, but I'm able to make it back to the bed before my jelly legs give out. I glance at the tray of tea and toast

Duke delivered as I sink onto the bed. I'll just sit for a few moments.

The next time I'm aware of my surroundings, nighttime has fallen, and it's dark outside the window walls. I'm once again covered, lying in the same unfamiliar bed, but this time I know I must be in a guest room at Duke's penthouse. Then I remember about Duke's finding my hiding place. And what am I going to do now that he has? How can I explain my homeless situation and still keep my dignity intact?

This time when I stand beside the bed, my head is a little muzzy, but I get my feet under me quickly. I make it to the bathroom, and the lure of the shower is simply too much to resist. I pull off my borrowed clothes, carefully fold them and put them on the marble counter, and turn the shower dial. Water shoots from a rain showerhead and six different body sprays. I sigh in sublime contentment as I stand under the warm, massaging water. Never have I felt so decadently pampered. The shower at our house in Jersey would have already run out of hot water, and if Dad turned the water on in the kitchen, a burst of cold water would douse you in shocking surprise.

I squirt out some bodywash and sniff. Sandalwood and vanilla, if I had to guess. *Ahh.* It feels so creamy and smooth against my skin. The next bottle holds shampoo. I inhale the lovely scent of lavender as I make quick work of lathering, rinsing, and repeating. The conditioner comes next, and my hair feels silky soft. I even used more body wash for a second cleaning, just because I didn't want to get out.

"What do you think you're doing?" a loud voice says as the glass shower door opens.

I scream, and my feet slip out from under me. A cold breeze hits me on my way to the marble tile floor, just before strong hands grab me. Dripping wet, Duke's arms hold me like steel bands tightly to his chest. I hear his heart-beat racing as quickly as mine.

"Are you all right?" Duke asks, his eyes searching my body for injury.

My nipples swell into tight buds. I'd like to think the reaction is from the cold, but I know it's not. "Yes, I'm fine. You startled me."

"I'm sorry. I came to check on you, and you weren't in bed. Then I heard the shower and thought you'd fallen." His voice sounds thick and husky.

"No. I'm fine." I bury my face against Duke's white t-shirt, now soaking wet. I breathe in his scent. More sandal-wood. It's becoming my favorite fragrance. As my senses return, I tip my head back and look up at Duke. He's slightly pale and perhaps even a bit in shock. Had he been that worried about me? Then I understand the intense look in his eyes. A very strange and unknown feeling unfurls inside me as I feel him harden against my stomach. "Duke..."

Kiss me. Kiss me. Kiss me. I chant in my head, luring him into a kiss I know we both want. We're so close, so tightly matched that I can feel his length growing against my belly. I can't think straight. All I can do is feel. Need. Want. When his lips are a mere breath from mine, blood rushes to my head. When he claims my lips, a whimper comes from my throat.

His tongue caresses mine, deepening the kiss as his hands inch their way up my ribs much too slowly. I want his hands on me. Touching me. Making me feels things I've never felt before. Never has a simple kiss made me lose control and my mind a total blank. When his hand cups my breast, I gasp. When his fingers tweak my nipple, I wanted to climb his body and sink down onto his hardness.

With a tortured moan, Duke tears his lips from mine and steps back, breaking our connection. His eyes roam over my body, and I melt under the close scrutiny of his gaze. I wobble from the intensity and he steadies me with a hand. Once I'm stable, he turns me loose like a hot potato. Quickly, he averts his eyes and grabs a towel from the warming rack on the wall and shoves it into my hands. "I'm sorry, Harlow. I didn't mean to—"

I wrap the towel around my body and touch his arm. What was I thinking? "It's okay, Duke."

He takes another step closer to the door and farther away from me. "I just thought you were in trouble."

I nod as I wonder if he's regretting that kiss. "I under-stand," I say, to give him an out.

"Please forgive the interruption," he says from the bath-room doorway.

"Of course." I noticed he said nothing about the kiss. I'm beginning to wonder if I imagined his lips on mine.

His head jerks into a stilted nod. "I'll have Ms. Bennett bring you something light to eat. You must be hungry," he says and then flies from the bathroom, without a backward glance.

I turn to the mirror, stunned by the look on my face. I raise my hand to touch my flushed cheek and then run my fingers over my puffy, swollen lips. Duke just saw me completely naked. He even held my naked body in his arms while he kissed me like nobody's business. Why am I not freaking out about that? And why am I disappointed we stopped?

CHAPTER SEVEN

Duke

Throwing my bathroom door open, I turn the cold water on in the shower and step in, clothes and all. I hiss at the biting cold, hoping my throbbing dick will get on board with not getting what he wants. I'd been so close to taking Harlow right there in the bathroom. What type of insensitive lout am I? The fact that she's a guest in my house—and ill—should have been enough of an impetus to keep myself in check. I peer down at my straining cock and turn the temperature control to the coldest setting.

I've resisted her for months, yet I still want her. Trying to convince myself to leave her alone is no longer working. I know what I am, and I know what's in my future, and no matter how incredibly alluring I find Harlow, I can't have her. I close my eyes, and I can feel her creamy skin against mine. I'd gone instantly hard. My thin silk pajama pants had done nothing to hide that fact. I push the wet garment down my legs and kick them to a corner of the shower. Bracing my hands against the tile wall, I dunk my head under the frigid spray.

Her kisses leave me wanting so much more. I'll never get the taste of her from my mouth. Sweet as sugar and as addictive as any vice. I groan from just the memory of her breast in my palm. My hand wraps around my erection as I relive the too-few moments I held her body. I begin to pump in a slow, desperate motion. I visualize what would have happened if I hadn't stepped back and left her alone.

In my mind, I see her lower to her knees before me. Her gentle hands wrap around me as her tongue peeks from between her lips and swipes away a drop of creamy liquid before taking me into her mouth. She strokes me with her hands and takes me deep. Her lips wrap around the base and she suckles me even deeper with each stroke. In my daydream, I hit the back of her throat.

A pressure begins to build in my lower spine. The rush of release is coming, and I welcome the relief. A deafening roar explodes in my head as I come against the shower wall. I growl as each spasm empties me but still leaves me wanting. *Harlow.*

"Bloody hell!" My shout vibrates off the tile walls surrounding me as I slap the water off, my breathing still labored. I must stop having these inappropriate fantasies. I need to remember that Harlow is a guest in my home.

The next morning, I find Harlow and Ms. Bennett chatting in the kitchen as I come down the stairs. When I round the corner, I'm surprised at finding Harlow dressed in the jeans and t-shirt she'd worn on our picnic and looking much better. There's still a slight shadow under her eyes, but without the weakness clouding her gaze. She notices me entering the room and smiles shyly, then she hides her face by looking down into her coffee cup, but not before I see embarrassment cross her face—whether from her reaction to our kiss or from her previous living arrangements, I can't say.

"Good morning, Harlow. Ms. Bennett," I say as I enter the room, and both women's heads turn in my direction.

"Morning, sir," Ms. Bennett replies.

"We'll be in the breakfast room when our food is ready." My eyes come to rest on Harlow, and I'm curious why she won't look at me.

"Certainly, sir. I'll have everything out shortly." Ms. Bennett nods and turns to prepare our meal.

Harlow still hasn't looked up from her investigation of the liquid inside her cup. "This way, Harlow." I step aside as she passes and walk behind her to the breakfast room. I smell her scent, and I'm right back where I was before:

wanting her. She goes straight to the windows and the view before her. I clear my throat and say, "I want to apologize for my behavior last night. I was completely out of line. I took advantage while you were ill. That was not well done of me."

Harlow turns. Our gazes meet, and I sense her confusion as she admits, "I didn't feel taken advantage of." Her honest reply astonishes me.

A blush blooms on her face, and I find it quite archaic that I find that satisfying. "Be that as it may, I do apologize."

We both look up as Ms. Bennett wheels a buffet cart into the room. I wait for Harlow to serve her plate, and then I take a soft-boiled egg, toast, and a cup of tea and join her at the table, where I'm happy to see she's already enjoying her food. "I'm glad to see your appetite has returned."

Her fork pauses in midair, then she places it on the plate and sighs. A long-suffering sigh. "Yes. Thank you. This is delicious. I'll get out of your hair as soon as I finish. Thanks for letting me recuperate here. That was very nice of you."

And that brings me right back to why she was living on the third floor. And from her expression, she's bracing for the inquisition. Keeping a neutral expression on my face and a non-judgmental tone to my voice, I ask, "How long have you been homeless?"

She jerks as if I've struck her then swallows, folding her hands in front of her. "I...um, don't really think of myself as homeless, but I guess that's exactly what I am. For about six months," she admits.

I rub my forehead. Six months she's been without a home. Anything could have happened to her, and that gives me cold chills. "And how did this happen?"

"I prefer not to say," she says quietly.

Stubborn. "You know I could have you arrested," I say bitingly, then regret my tone when her head snaps up. She looks positively terrified.

"You—"

I hold my hand up, putting a quick end to my threat. "But I won't." I rub the back of my neck, feeling a headache coming on. "I will assume you are going through a rough patch in your life."

She shrugs and nods. "You could say that. I've almost saved enough for first and last month's rent at Amber Ridge Apartments."

There's no way I'll allow her to live in those apartments. Most of them should be condemned. "What do you plan on doing in the meantime?"

Her mouth twists up into a hopeful, lopsided grin. "Well, would you allow me to live on the third floor?"

Oh, no. That's not happening. "I can't see that happening. One of the reasons you were so sick was because you spent the night in near-freezing conditions after being doused in the river. In fact, I've already had all of your things removed, and the room is now demolished." Her lower lip begins to tremble, and I feel like a cad.

"You...you had no right to do that," she says with emotionless desolation.

I narrow my eyes. Obviously, she's forgotten who owns White Oaks. "I believe I do. I own the building you've been living in rent-free. Had you been found by the fire inspector, I could have been shut down or lost my license completely." That last part was probably overkill, but I need her safe.

Her eyes lower, but not before I see them fill with tears. "I'm sorry. I didn't know. I'll just be going now," she says, pushing to her feet.

"Sit down," I order sharply. She falls back into the chair, and I finally see a spark of irritation shining in her eyes. I knew she was in there. "You aren't going anywhere. I've had all your things moved into my guest suite. You will stay there until your finances improve." I still don't know how that happened. I had been arranging for her to move into a vacant apartment, but then I told Ms. Bennett to move her into the guest room she'd been staying in.

"What?" she shouts, shooting to her feet and shaking her head. "No, Duke. I can't stay here."

"Why not?" I cross my arms and wait for her reply, curious as to why her cheeks flushed pink.

"Because...because..." she stutters.

"Good. That's decided, then," I say, and my lips tip into a grin as she cuts her eyes to me. "You will stay here, but I'm afraid Amber Ridge isn't acceptable housing. When you're ready, I'll have a unit prepared for you here."

She blinks with a dazed look. "But that will take me

over a year to save for. You can't want me to stay here that long."

I take my time spreading jam on my toast before I answer. Because yes, I do want her to stay, and I forget all about the reasons she shouldn't. "I see no reason why you can't. I have the room, and it's not being used."

She blinks, her eyes glazing over in confusion. "But won't I cramp your style or something?"

"Cramp my style?" My eyes pull together. "Is this an American expression?" I ask.

She purses her lips in frustration and explains, "When you invite female guests to your home."

"That shan't be an issue. I never invite guests back to my home," I admit. Spending time with women has never been an issue, but I never bring them home. My home is my refuge. Yet, I don't mind that Harlow is here. I want her here.

Now it's Harlow's turn to look muddled. "You don't? Where do you…you know?" Her cheeks flush.

I know what she's asking, but I'm curious how she'll explain it to me. "No. Obviously I don't know."

"You never bring your dates here to… spend the night?" she nervously asks.

Her cheeks glow such a pretty shade of pink. "Sex is what you're referring to?" I ask, mostly to see her reaction.

Her head bobs as she plays with her napkin. "Well, yes."

"I can assure you, I've never had issues in the past. It's settled, then. You will stay here. I also took the liberty of adding a few pieces to your wardrobe. Since I have no idea what happened in your life, I must assume that you're also in need of clothing."

"My clothes were—are... I do have clothes. A whole wardrobe. Or at least I did. I just don't have any idea where my things are now." Her eyes go back to her hands.

Whatever happened is upsetting to her. Without knowing, my mind goes to scenarios that chill me to the bone. "Harlow. We've known each other for months now. I'd like to think we've become friends. Tell me what happened. Let me help you."

She stares into my eyes. "We are friends, Duke. But you can't help me. Nobody can help me."

I hold her gaze. "Are you in trouble? Is anyone looking for you?"

"No. Nothing like that." She pauses, and I can see her weighing exactly how much to tell me. "My father and I were relocating to Tennessee, and he needed to leave suddenly."

Her father? "Okay. But why did you find yourself homeless?"

Again, she pauses. "He left in such a hurry, and he took all my things and all the money I'd saved with him in the trailer we'd rented."

My anger rises as I think of all that could have happened to Harlow. "Your father left you homeless and destitute?" *What type of man is he?*

She is quick to defend her father. "I'm sure he didn't mean to. He just wasn't thinking clearly at the time."

I notice there's something in her eyes. Something that she's not saying. "Is your father ill? Does he have dementia?" I ask, because that's the only way I can justify his actions.

She pauses a bit too long before answering. "No. Nothing like that. He's had problems since my mom died."

I remember her telling me about her mom's death, but. "Wasn't that years ago?"

She nods, "Yes, when I was sixteen. But he's never been the same since."

My hands tighten into fists, my jaw clenches, and I ask, "Was your father abusive to you?" I hold my breath for her answer.

Her eyes pop open, and she shakes her head. "No, never. Just forgetful sometimes."

I can tell she loves her father even after what he did. I can only imagine what she's gone through. I have a great respect and admiration for her strength. "Forgetful? How?" I push for more.

"Mom always handled everything around the house. Sometimes he'd forget to buy food, or pay the bills." I see hesitation in her eyes.

I know there's more she's not saying, but I need to remember she is recovering from being ill. Her eyes show me she's exhausted. I shouldn't have kept her up and talking this long. She needs rest. "I see. Well, for now, you'll stay here. I need to get to work. I've already called Kaylee and told her you wouldn't be in for the rest of the week."

"Duke, no. I can't do that. I'm fine. It was just a cold," she says, but there's no fight left in her.

"A cold where you ran a 102-degree temperature. You need rest and good food to set you right. Ms. Bennett is here if you need anything. Tell her what you'd like for lunch, and she will prepare whatever you want." I pause on the way out. "I had your jewelry studio set up in the conservatory. I thought you'd like the light there." I don't wait for her response. Before I leave, I stop by the kitchen and ask Ms. Bennett to help Harlow back to bed. I wanted to carry her in my arms, but I thought it best for my sanity to escape while I could.

CHAPTER EIGHT

Harlow

"Ms. Davidson, may I get you anything else?"

Ms. Bennett snaps me out of the funk I'd been in since Duke made his decree and then breezed off to work. I don't understand why he's acting this way. Yes, he'd seen me naked. Yes, we'd kissed twice. But that still didn't explain why he was acting all possessive toward me.

"No, thank you, Ms. Bennett. Breakfast was delicious. I think I'll go to my room and rest for a while."

"Certainly, dear. Mr. Ainsworth was concerned you'd overextended this morning. Shall I bring your lunch up later?"

I smile. She reminds me so much of my mom. "Here

will be nice, thank you." I didn't want to make extra work for her.

"Mr. Ainsworth asked me to give you this. He said he's already added contact information for himself as well as for your friends," she says, handing me a new phone and charger. She leaves before I can wrap my brain around the fact that I'm holding the newest model available. My old phone had been several versions old and had been free with the lowest monthly plan I could afford.

I laugh at the sticky note attached to the screen. "Sorry your birthday gift is late." And he'd used my birth date as the password. My eyes begin to sting when I push the button to turn the phone on and the home screen is a picture of a birthday cake with balloons and streamers. He'd gone to so much trouble and had put a lot of thought into the gift. I don't know how I feel about this.

As I leave the breakfast room and make my way upstairs, I can't believe the grandeur of Duke's home. I have no idea what it would feel like to live in a place like this. Safe for sure. As always, my eyes go to the massive windows in each room and the grand mountains in the distance. The leaves are just starting to turn. In a few weeks, the view will be incredible when they're at their peak color. Will I still be here to enjoy them? I don't know, and suddenly I feel extremely insecure.

Once I'm in my room, I go straight to my closet and walk into a room the size of my bedroom in Jersey. My eyes grow larger and more disbelieving the further in I go. "Add a few things..." I mumble what Duke had said. What I'm looking at is much more than a few things. I touch a silky yellow blouse and hold it to my face. I read the tag. Silk. Where did he think I would wear clothes like these? I finger the dresses, skirts, dress slacks, blouses, and jackets all hanging by style and color. There're even coats—dress coats and North Face jackets. I've never had a dress coat, and North Face has never been an option for me.

In a drawer, I find a rainbow of bras and panties from a brand I'd never heard of before, but they're obviously expensive. The next drawer holds workout clothes, and I laugh. Other than attending a few free Zumba classes in my early twenties, I've never had time or money to go to a gym. I did enjoy running in high school, but I was working so many jobs I couldn't keep my place on the track team. Then, later, I'd always be too tired to go for a run.

I close that drawer and open the next and find six pairs of folded jeans. Six! I pull a pair out and hold the soft cotton to my face. I never knew jeans could feel so soft. These aren't like the big-box-store jeans I usually buy. These are designer, and I'd be much too nervous that I'd ruin them to wear them. The bottom drawer holds tank tops and t-shirts.

I pull my new phone from my back pocket and type out a quick text to Duke.

A few clothes? I add a thinking face emoji. I wait for a response, unsure if I'll even get a reply. Three dots pop up, showing he's typing, and my heart jumps.

Are they to your liking?

I roll my eyes and type, *How could they not be?*
You should be resting.

I laugh and reply, *I just wanted to say thank you for my*
birthday gift. For the clothes and a place to live and for
being my friend. I think about the last part and then delete
everything except *I just wanted to say thank you,* before
pushing send.

Go rest.

I send back a pouty face emoji and close my phone with
a smile.

I step back and take in the closet's contents. I'm speechless. I've never had so many clothes in my life. I can't
believe Duke did all this. For me. Why? I don't know, and
I'm too tired to figure it out now. I pull on a pair of yoga
pants and a tank top from the closet. I bypass looking in the
mirror and fall face-first on the bed.

That night, I'm waiting on Duke in the living room when he
gets home from work. Which is funny to me because his
office is just downstairs. He rides an elevator to work each
day. I'm wearing one of the dresses from my fairytale closet
stash. It's a mustard-gold wrap dress with blue and terra
cotta flowers. It's a very demure style, but it fits me like a
glove. I'd left my hair down, blowing it dry and letting it
fall into curly waves around my shoulders. I used some of
the new makeup I'd found in the bathroom. Just a swipe of

blush, lip gloss, and a bit of mascara. Honestly, I have no idea how to use the rest of the bottles and tubes. Paired with the sexy lingerie I'm wearing underneath, I feel pretty and feminine, something I've not felt in a very long time—if ever.

As soon as Duke sees me, he stops, but his eyes roam my body, taking in my new dress and making me feel appreciated and tingly inside.

"Hi," I say breathlessly.

"Good evening, Harlow. You look beautiful," he says in a throaty voice, his attention focused on my lips. Nervously, I run my tongue over my bottom lip, and Duke's eyes darken. His reaction makes me feel like a desirable woman, something I've never felt before. Even the few relationships I've had over the years have never made me feel as wanted.

"Thank you," I say and take a shuddering breath, letting my eyes drink him in. Duke is so handsome in his charcoal suit and buttery yellow tie. My gaze stops on his tie, and in my mind, I see that tie against my skin. My hand goes to my neck, and I tug on the coral-and-silver necklace I'd worn, trying to get more air into my lungs. My gaze moves slowly upward and connects with his, and I almost incinerate from the burn I find there. Then, just as quickly, it's gone.

It's like a shutter slammed down on his emotions, and he's back to being distant and polite. "Did you work on your jewelry pieces today?" he asks.

I try to catch up, but I'm feeling a bit lost. I can't turn

my feelings off as quickly as he did. "No. I didn't know where they were, and I didn't want to bother Ms. Bennett."

Duke pinches the bridge of his nose and looks like he may be counting to ten. "I'll show you after dinner. Come, let's eat." Duke put his hand in the small of my back and then stops and looks down. "Where are your shoes?"

I feel myself blush. "Um, I'm not used to wearing heels, and there weren't any flats. I didn't think my tennis shoes would really go with this dress so..." I look down and wiggle my toes.

I glance up and see a smile tug at the corner of his lips, and that little break in his facade is enough to give me hope that what we felt earlier wasn't one-sided. "Fine. Let's eat."

Duke pulls out my chair, and I push my hair back behind my ears in a nervous tic. I'm not familiar with such a gallant and polite act. "Did you have a good day?" I ask.

"Yes. Very productive," he says and picks up his fork.

The aroma coming from my plate makes my stomach growl. How embarrassing. I look up quickly, but Duke is still focused on eating. This is the first time my appetite is back since being ill. The mashed potatoes are creamy and smooth. The beef roast is tender and juicy. My chewing slows, and I tip my head. I can't remember the last time I had such a delicious home-cooked meal. Probably when my mom was alive. I feel a pressure behind my eyes, and I lay my fork down beside my plate. Missing my mom hasn't hit me so hard in years.

"What's wrong, Harlow? You seem sad."

My eyes move to his, finding his gaze filled with concern. How did he pick up on my emotion so quickly? I sigh and lean back in my seat. "No, not sad. Just sentimental, maybe. I was thinking of the last time I had such a delicious home-cooked meal. It was when my mom was alive. She made the best mashed potatoes, and her biscuits were so light and fluffy."

"You don't cook?" he asks.

I laugh, remembering some of the inedible meals I'd made. "Not with much success. But I can box cook," I tell him with a teasing grin.

His brows pull together in confusion. "Box cook?"

I smile. Not all times with Dad were bad. "Yeah, if I can buy it in a box where I have the directions, at least my dad and I can eat it. Truthfully, we mostly ate takeout. I'd grab something on the way home between jobs. I suppose I should have paid more attention to my mom when she cooked."

"Were you close to your mother?" Duke asks and waits with interest in his eyes for my answer.

I nod, feeling a bit emotional. "Yes, she was my best friend." I blink to chase away the tears I feel building behind my eyes. "I was close to both of my parents."

"I'm sure you miss her," Duke says. His eyes focus on mine as I try to regain my composure, and I see nothing but compassion in his gaze.

I tell him honestly, "I miss them both."

"You said your dad changed after your mom passed?"

Duke leans forward and rests his crossed arms on the table. He's completely absorbed in our conversation, and that touches me.

"It was like I lost them both on the same day. Dad was there with me, but he wasn't. Do you know what I mean? It felt like our roles were reversed." I look up and catch his eyes—he does understand. He lost his father.

His face takes on a faraway look as he remembers his own loss. "My mother went through the normal grief period, if there is such a thing, when my father died. She still has days when I know she's sad. They were married for over thirty years. Recently, she's even started seeing a gentleman friend in the village."

I grin. He doesn't seem very happy that his mother is dating. "Your mom sounds like a lovely woman."

"She is," he says. "But she can be difficult to get along with."

Difficult? That could mean many things. I'm glad I'll never have the opportunity to meet her. The rest of our dinner conversation consists of many varied topics. From what our next book study should be, to the popularity of my tea charms, and to back-and-forth games of 'What is your favorite…'

Finally, Duke pushes back from the table and says, "Come, let me show you your studio."

As we leave the dining room, Duke's hand rests on the small of my back once again. The warmth of his hand seeps through the fabric of my dress. I want to turn around and melt into his arms and kiss him again like we did the night before.

We walk upstairs, down a hallway, and then up another flight of stairs before walking into a room surrounded by floor-to-ceiling windows. I think this must be the highest point in the entire town of Treemont. "This is incredible," I say as I spin around, taking in the view from each direction. The lights of Treemont sparkle in the north windows. I can only imagine how beautiful the view of the mountains must be during the day. I'd been so engrossed in the windows I hadn't even noticed the worktable with my supplies already set up and organized. "Where did these bins and storage drawers come from?"

Duke looks a bit uncomfortable admitting, "I had Ms. Sheldon order what one would have in a jewelry studio. I hope everything meets with your approval."

I point toward my beat-up tackle box. "But I only had that one box full of supplies."

"Yes, well, I thought maybe you could use a few more things. If something isn't to your liking, simply ask Ms. Sheldon to return it."

I picked up a roll of wire. "This is silver." I say in awe. I've never been able to afford the high grade. My mind goes crazy with design ideas I can make.

"Yes. Is that wrong?" he asks, stepping closer.

I can feel his body heat and smell the sandalwood scent from his soap. "No, not wrong, just incredibly expensive. It's real silver. I've never worked with the real thing."

I open a drawer marked *Gemstones* and gasp. "Duke! These are real gemstones."

Another drawer holds silversmithing tools: soldering irons, paste, flux, torches, stamps and punches, cutting tools, anvils and blocks. I even see things that I have no idea what their purpose is. While I have done some silver work, it was always much too expensive to play around with. And that's all my jewelry-making has ever been. I'm totally baffled why he bought me all these things. "Duke...why? Why did you do all this?"

He brushes my hair back and runs his thumb over my jaw. I shiver from his touch. "This is important to you," he says.

I nod and move away so I can breathe without wanting to wrap myself in his arms. "It is. My mom designed and created pieces. All I have was once hers. Well, as much as I could bring with me."

"I've seen your work, Harlow. You have talent as well. I especially love the suncatcher you made for my office."

I grin. Yeah, I knew I wasn't pulling anything past him with my little offerings to make his office not quite so stuffy. But I still won't admit his secret fairy is me. "I don't know what you're talking about."

He chuckles and nods. "Whatever you say."

His eyes take on a teasing glint, and I laugh and say, "Thank you, Duke." His eyes capture mine, and I see I've made him happy by accepting his generosity. I only hope he knows he would have my gratitude simply by being him.

"You're very welcome, Harlow."

Later, as I lay in bed, I know that today was the probably the best day of my life. So what if I'm the only one who considered it a date?

The next morning, I'm sitting at the breakfast table by myself. Ms. Bennett said Duke had an overseas conference call and had already left for work. I wish I'd been able to see him this morning. I sigh as I take another bite of Ms. Bennett's delicious, fluffy eggs and crispy bacon. I'm going to miss this. And I will be leaving, so I need to remember that and not get too attached. Not only to the comforts Duke's home provides, but to the man himself.

"Excuse me, Harlow. You have a phone call," Ms. Bennett says, handing me a cordless phone.

"Thank you." I stare at the phone, wondering who could be calling. Then I chuckle. I could just answer it and find out. "Hello, this is Harlow."

"Harlow! Please, I need your help!" A very frantic Rachael pleads.

"Rach, slow down. What do you need?" I ask.

"I called Kaylee. She told me where you were, and we will definitely discuss that later. She said you've been sick, so it's okay if you don't feel well enough, but my food truck is scheduled to be in Asheville today for a Care Meals day, and Kyle and I are stuck in California. I thought we'd get there in time. Can you take over for me?" she asks hopefully.

Me, prepare food? I want to laugh. Kyle surprised Rachael with a food truck. Rachael, being the incredible, giving woman that she is, has begun providing Care Meals for the homeless in surrounding areas as much as she can. I'll feel really bad if I can't help her, but I don't want to make the homeless sick.

"Take over for you? What does that mean?" I ask cautiously. I wasn't lying when I told Duke I couldn't cook. If she expects me to man the grill, there will be a lot of disappointed people.

"I promise it will be super easy. I have several area restaurants donating food that's already prepared, and the truck is already being delivered to the site. All you have to do is hand out the food," she explains.

"That sounds like something I can handle. I have a phone now, so let me give you the number and just text me the details."

After we chat a bit longer, I rush upstairs and pull out a new pair of jeans, but then I stop and think about who I'll be serving and I return them to their crisply folded state and scrounge around for my own jeans. But I can't help myself, and I grab a new dark green t-shirt that says *"Over it"* on the front.

After letting Ms. Bennett know where I'm going, it hits me that I have no way of getting to Asheville. I could Uber, but an hour-long trip will eat up a big chunk of my savings.

As much as I don't want to, I stop by Duke's office to see if I can borrow his car. I'd never ask for myself, but this is a really good cause.

I step off the elevator, and Ms. Sheldon looks up from her computer with a smile. "Hello, Harlow. Are you feeling better?"

"Yes, I feel much better. Thank you. I was wondering if Duke would have time to see me. Just for a few minutes." I've never just stopped by to see him. I feel nervous. What if he's busy or I interrupt him?

"Of course, dear. Just let me ring him. I believe he's finished his call." She wasn't on the phone but a second before she nodded toward the office door. "Just go right on in."

I find Duke behind his desk, holding the dog figurine I'd secretly given him. I'd found it at a second-hand store for a quarter. It had reminded me of a story he had told me about his childhood dog. I can see how much he likes it, and that makes me happy. I explain to Duke about Rachael's call and ask to borrow a car, then somehow, we are both in the back of his car with Jeffrey driving us both to Asheville. I can only imagine how this is going to look to the people who come for free food.

I sigh and narrow my eyes, still irritated he wouldn't let me go alone. Who am I kidding? I love that he wanted to join me. "I still say I'm perfectly healthy."

From the look in his eyes, I know he won't be moved to change his mind. "You may be, but this sounds like it could be too taxing for you. I will feel much better if I'm there to help."

I cross my arms and turn my head to grin. "Fine, but you're going to have to do something about what you're wearing."

"What's wrong with my suit?" he asks, and tugging at his shirt cuffs.

Nothing if you're on the Fortune 500 list, I think to myself. "The people we're going to see today won't be dressed for business."

He takes a moment to think. "I see what you mean." He nods and takes his jacket off. "There. Is that better?"

"Keep going. Lose the tie and cufflinks." I watch his tie slide from around his neck, and naughty thoughts fill my mind as he rolls his sleeves up, revealing toned, firm forearms. I've been fantasizing about his ties.

"Harlow?"

His raised voice snaps me out of the lust-filled fog I'd created. "What?"

He grins and repeats, "I asked if there is anything else you'd like me to remove?"

Oh boy, is there. My gaze flashes to his, and I see a mischievous smirk on his face. He knows what I was thinking about. My hand goes to my cheek. It's warm and, I'm sure, red. I clear my throat and smile. "That should do it."

By midafternoon, I'm glad Duke decided to come. Even

Jeffrey volunteered his help. More than once I've caught myself watching Duke as he interacts with the men and women who slowly trickled in throughout the afternoon. It was like he took off his reserved, British businessman aspect along with his suit coat and tie. He'd even handed out his card to several people after having a conversation with them. I'm not sure what that's about, but I have a feeling he's going to help them in some way. I don't think he sees himself as compassionate, but that's what he's done with his energy conservation efforts, and it's what he's doing now. I'm sure not a single person he served today thought of him as a billionaire.

I admit to myself that Duke isn't anything like I thought he was, and I like the man he is. Not because of what he did for me but because he cares deeply and wants to make things better for everyone. I don't think he realizes that about himself.

The next morning, Duke reluctantly allows me to go back to work. As soon as I walk in, Kaylee gives me a very smug 'I told you so' look.

"So, you're staying with Mr. Ainsworth?" she says, and her lips and brow slide into a smirk as she crosses her arms and waits for me to explain.

And how am I going to explain? "He was very thoughtful by letting me recuperate there. I guess since I passed out in his office, he felt responsible."

"Sure he did," she says, but she doesn't look the least bit convinced.

I shrug and try to walk by her to go to the back, but she blocks my exit. "What do you want me to say?"

"I see the way he looks at you, Harlow. And I see the way you look at him when you don't think he's watching. You can't tell me there's nothing going on between you two."

I sigh and fall into a chair at one of the customer tables. Kaylee plops a cup of my favorite tea in front of me and takes a seat. "Harlow, what's going on? Tell me, sweetie. Let me help you."

The love and understanding in her voice touches something inside me. I've never had someone who cared enough to want to help. "You're right. I do have feelings for Duke. Hopelessly impossible feelings."

Her brows draw together, and she asks, "Why impossible?"

I give her a half laugh. "Oh, come on, Kay. It's pretty obvious."

Her chin rises. "You better not be thinking you're not good enough for him. I'll tear you a new one."

Her attempt at fierceness makes me smile. "I just don't see a future with Duke."

The look on her face says she doesn't believe me. "So, nothing has happened between you two?"

"No. Not really. I mean we've kissed twice." I'm not mentioning one of those was in the shower. That sounds worse that it really was. "He's asked me to move in."

Her eyes grow large, and her grin returns. "What? Why didn't you say that first?"

I shrug and try to pass it off as nothing of importance. "Because it's not what you're thinking. I've been having some problems with where I've been living, and he offered to let me stay with him. Platonically," I add, to take away any possibilities of her misunderstanding.

Her eyes narrow in on my face. She must decide I'm telling the truth, because she sighs and says, "You should have said something. You could have stayed with me."

And that's exactly why I didn't tell her. "I know. Thanks. But this is my problem," I tell her, then I head to the back to get ready for the day.

She halts me with a hand on arm. "Harlow. Don't sell yourself short. I think there's something between you two."

I have to admit it. "I feel it, too. But I don't think it's smart to act on those feelings. I'll only end up getting hurt."

"Oh, sweetie. I'm here for you if you need to talk. But I just want you to consider giving whatever is between you two a chance."

I smile and nod, knowing it's fruitless even to consider a future with Duke. This time I do make it back into the kitchen, where I start prepping for the day. Kaylee follows me in.

"Now, I don't want you to freak out, but I have some exciting news to tell you." She speaks calmly but fights to keep her composure.

I look up from the teapot I'm filling with water. "Oookay," I cautiously say. It's the word 'freak' that has me concerned. The animated look on her face has me afraid of what's coming.

She puts her palms flat on the table to keep herself grounded as she explains. "April had a guy they work with on the show create a website for you," she says, looking like she's about to burst with excitement.

April and her husband Elias host a home renovation television show for a major network. Why would she do that? My head tips, and my brows draw together. That's certainly not what I imagined her saying. "Huh? A website? Why do I need a website?"

She takes a breath, and her smile grows exponentially as she says, "Well, April had him put your tea charms and some of your jewelry up for sale."

My eyes bulge, and I can't get them to blink. "What?" I shout.

Kaylee holds her hands up like a stop sigh. "Just wait. That's not the freak-out part. You've only been live for two days, and you've already sold over five hundred tea charms!" She squeals in giddiness, jumps from her seat, and wraps her arms around me, dragging my tremoring body up.

I'm speechless. All I can say is, "What?"

Quickly, she stops her happy dance and adds, "Don't worry. Baylee and I will help you make them. We'll close early one day and set up an assembly line."

My mind is spinning, trying to do the math. That's... that's... I gasp, grab the table, and slowly lower myself to the chair before my legs give out. Do I have enough supplies? I'll have to order them. Thank goodness I have a bit of savings.

Kaylee stops her celebration and asks, "Harlow, talk to me. You're scaring me."

I just shake my head. I can't believe it. "I…I don't know what to say. I never imagined anyone would be interested in buying them. I suppose I need to create an inventory. And I bet there's something I need to do business-wise." I rub my forehead, feeling a stress headache coming on.

She nods then gets a devious look in her eyes. "Ask Duke to help you."

She doesn't give up. "I guess I could." I'm hesitant to ask him. He manages billion-dollar deals; my small venture would be a joke to him. Not even worth his efforts.

I don't know how I feel about this windfall. Grateful, certainly, but I'm not sure I should put much trust into making money from something so simple. I'll fill the orders and just see what happens.

CHAPTER NINE

Duke

"Send the entire packet of documents to legal," I say as my eyes move to the sunlight coming through the window behind her. It's probably one of the last sunny days we'll have for a while.

"Right away. Is that all?" Ms. Sheldon asks as she gathers the documents we'd been going over.

My pen taps a happy rhythm on my desktop. "Yes, that's all. Why don't you take off early today?"

The shock that comes over her face lets me know that I've been lacking in this area.

"If you're sure, sir?" she asks, giving me a wide opening to change my mind.

I nod and grin when the door closes. I've never seen Ms. Sheldon at a loss for words. I swivel my chair around and gaze out the windows at the mountain view. I've begun to enjoy spending too much time daydreaming at that view. I have Harlow to thank for bringing it to my attention.

Living with Harlow the past few weeks has been nice. Very nice. Something that I could get used to easily. After my inappropriate advances, our relationship has slipped back into friendship. At least that's how it appears on the surface. The more time I spend around her, though, the more I want her. I'm back to fighting my attraction to her and taking cold showers. But it's worth it to be around her.

I've seen her luscious body, and I can't put that vision back in the box. I've held her breast in my hand and my mouth waters for a taste. I begin to swell, which has been a common occurrence lately when I'm near Harlow or simply thinking of her.

My cellphone rings, and I turn back around, leaving the view and my thoughts of Harlow behind. I smile when I see my mum's picture on the screen.

"Hello, Mum." I lean my head back and stare at the ceiling. I know this won't be a short chat.

"Oliver, dear, I have the most exciting news."

I grin, wondering whose done what with whom now. "I can't wait to hear."

"Alyssa Pendwick is home from Italy. I think you should invite her to your cousin's wedding," she announces.

Like bloody hell I will. I sit up straighter. Alyssa is a

leech. I made the mistake of being with her in my early twenties. Once. That was enough to know she had her sights set on being Lady Ainsworth. There is no way I want to put myself through that again. "That's wonderful, Mum, but I already have a plus-one for the wedding," comes spewing from my mouth, and I have no idea why.

"You do?" Her voice fills with hopeful excitement. "Why haven't you said anything? Who is she?"

I can almost see her glowing with excitement through the phone. I rub the back of my neck to relieve the tension my lie has suddenly caused. "Her name is Harlow, and we've been seeing each other for over six months now." Technically, that's true.

"Oliver, why am I just now finding out about this? Who is her family?" she says with that disapproving Mum voice.

"They're Americans, Mum. That doesn't really matter over here, and I can't imagine you would know them." The more I think about it, the more it seems that inviting Harlow is perfect.

She sighs and admits, "Probably not. But that doesn't matter; I'm sure she's wonderful. Can you come early and spend a few days with me before the parties begin? I'd love to meet your girlfriend."

Girlfriend. I should probably correct her. I open my mouth to do just that, but instead, I say, "I don't know. I'll have to look at our schedules and see if we're free."

"You must, Oliver. You simply must. Oh, Oliver, you've made me so happy, darling."

I should be ashamed of lying to my mum. But the thought of not having to deal with the women she says are perfect to be my wife somehow outweighs my little fib. Little? "Let me talk with Harlow, and I'll get back with you."

I hang up and drop my head into my hands. What am I going to do now? It's not that I don't want Harlow to attend with me. She would make the entire week bearable. But there are so many issues. The biggest one of all is that Harlow has no idea that Duke isn't my name or that I'm not only the Duke of Ainsworth, but the wedding I'll be attending is for my cousin, the prince. And then there's my mum. Once she meets Harlow, I know her approval will bottom out, and that's not fair to Harlow. I love my mum, but I know her. She can be...difficult.

By the time I walk into my home after work, I have a somewhat tentative plan, which all depends on Harlow. As has become our routine for the past few weeks, Harlow gets home from work before I do and works on her designs and her tea charms inventory. I take a few moments to change from my suit into casual slacks and a button-up shirt then meet Harlow in the den for drinks before Ms. Bennett serves dinner.

I pause in the doorway just to soak up the beautiful sight. And I'm not talking about the mountain view. Tonight, she's wearing a midnight-blue off-the-shoulder dress, and my fingers itch to see if one tug would expose what I already know to be an exquisite body. Then my brow arches in concern. Harlow stands at the window, lost in her thoughts with a sad, almost apprehensive look on her face. I know there are things she's not telling me. I've considered hiring an investigator to look into the matter. If she's in trouble, I want to help. I want to keep her safe. The whole story about her father leaving her doesn't make sense. I want to respect her privacy, but it's hard when her safety may be at stake.

She turns, and her face lights up when she sees me. "Hi. I didn't hear you come in."

My heart swells, and like I've been doing for weeks, I lock down my emotions. "I just got here. Is something wrong?" I ask gently, hoping she will share whatever has caused her to look so sad.

Nervously, she wrings her delicate hands together. "I need to ask you something, but you've already done so much."

"Harlow, you know you can ask me anything." Absolutely anything.

Her worried eyes find mine. "It's just that I feel like I'll be using you because it's such a minor thing compared to what you usually deal with."

I bite my lip. She has no idea how much I'd be willing to do for her. "What is it?"

She pauses then says, "A few weeks ago, April had a website created for my tea charms and jewelry."

I do believe I recommended a website a long time ago. Why didn't I just go ahead and do it? "Really? That's a wonderful idea. Don't worry if you're not selling much to start off with. It takes time to establish yourself as a business."

She presses her lips together and shakes her head. "It's not that. They're doing very well." She manages a small smile before continuing. "So well that I don't know what to do. I'm having problems keeping up with the orders. And Kaylee says I need to set up a business, but I have no idea how to do that."

I've had women ask me for jewels and trips abroad, but never have I had such a simple yet meaningful request. Watching Harlow become a successful businesswoman will be a very rewarding experience. "Is that why you've been working such long hours in your studio?"

She nods.

"And you want my help?" I ask.

Her smile brightens my evening as she answers. "Yes. Please."

I grin, feeling her excitement. "Say no more. I'll take care of everything."

Her smile falls, her chin rises, and she quickly says, "No, I want to learn how to do it. I mean, I worked on keeping the books at a garage. I know a little, but I need you to teach me the rest. I need to be able to sustain this business myself."

A commendable request that makes me proud of her. "Okay. That sounds doable. We'll start tomorrow when you bring our tea."

Her smile returns. "Thank you."

That brings me back to my problem. Talk about using someone; I'll be doing exactly that. Yet I'm going to do it anyway. "Now I have a favor to ask you."

Her eyes sparkle with interest. "Of course. Anything."

"Later. Are you ready for dinner, or would you like a drink first?" I ask.

"Dinner, please," she says. "I only had a muffin for lunch." To emphasize the point, her stomach chooses that moment to growl. Her smile becomes contagious as she walks toward me.

"After you." I step aside and let her pass. Her fragrance lingers in her path, and I breathe her in.

Once we're seated and served, I ask, "How was your day?"

She chuckles as she picks up her fork. "Busy. A busload of tourists stopped by on their way to Biltmore House. They kept us hopping. I bet I served over a hundred cups of tea today. How was your day?"

I wonder if this is how it would be when I marry. Will I be as interested in my wife's day as I am with Harlow's? "Good. My mum called."

"Oh, how is she?" Harlow asks and takes a sip of her wine.

I've discovered when Harlow drinks even a few sips of wine, her face and neck turn a very pretty shade of pink. I keep my gaze on her blooming cheeks. "She sounded well. She was very excited because she wanted me to invite

Alyssa Pendwick to my cousin's wedding," I say distastefully.

Harlow laughs and covers her mouth with her napkin. "I'm sorry, I didn't mean to laugh, but your face...I take it you don't want to invite Alyssa Pendwick?"

"I shudder at the thought, actually," I say bluntly.

She giggles again and gives me a very phony sympathetic grin. "Well, I'm sure your mother will understand."

My eyebrows go up. "Oh, she's fine with it, actually."

She takes a bite and swallows before saying, "See? That's good. She's not forcing a date on you."

"Umm... She's fine with it because I told her I already had a date for the wedding." I watched her face closely, and Harlow isn't thrilled at my mention of a date. *Interesting.* She moves her potatoes and peas together on her plate, which is strange, because Harlow doesn't like peas.

"That's nice. Is it anyone your mother knows?" she says and takes a sudden interest in her roasted vegetables.

I chuckle to myself and answer. "No, she's never met her. She's American."

Her head pops up, and her smile dims. "Oh. Okay. Is it anyone I know?"

I nod and pick up my glass. "I would say so." I pause to take a drink, swallow, and then slowly place my glass carefully on the table before I say, "I told Mum you were my date."

"That's nice." Harlow says and spears a carrot. Then her

head shoots up, and her fork clatters to the table. "You did what?" she shouts.

I place my silverware back on the table because I know this stubborn woman. This won't be an easily won battle, but I will win. I give her my best smile and say, "That's the favor I wanted to ask you. Harlow, would you please attend my cousin's boring wedding with me?"

Her lips pull at a smile, but she answers, "No," as she repeatedly shakes her head. "No. No. No."

Well, that won't do. "Can you give me one reason why you won't do this favor for me?" I push.

Her eyes narrowed in ire. "Well, for one thing, it's in England, and I don't have a passport."

I wave a hand in dismissal. "That's easily sorted. I can have one for you before we leave. And as far as proper dress for the events, I'll cover all of those, since you'd be doing this huge favor for me."

She worries her bottom lip, trying to come up with another excuse. "Can't you ask someone else?"

I nod. "I could, but I want to go with you," I insist.

"Duke…" she lets my name fade away, not yet willing to surrender. But I can see she's tempted.

Just like I know she's not telling me everything about her father, I know there's another reason why she doesn't want to go. "What, Harlow? What's the real reason?"

She looks down at her hands. "I don't mean this in a rude way, but we both know I'm not someone you'd ever choose to spend time with."

"Harlow, look at me please." I wait until I have her eyes. She's hurt by that admission, and I don't like that she thinks it's true. "I disagree. Haven't we gotten along swimmingly so far?"

She sighs, and her shoulders droop. "Until a few weeks ago, I was homeless."

"That wasn't your fault. I hold your father responsible for that," I bite out between gritted teeth. I'm still upset with the man.

"Maybe, but he couldn't help it. That's beside the point. You're crazy, you know that, right? There's no way I will fit in with your crowd."

"You don't give yourself enough credit. I think it's the other way 'round. My 'crowd,' as you call them, aren't good enough for you." I know what I'm asking her to walk into. My peers can be difficult, especially when they smell someone beneath them. But Harlow will be my guest, and I'll insist she's treated accordingly.

I go to her, take her hand, pull her from her chair, and look into her eyes. "Harlow, if you don't want to go, I'll accept that. But don't say no because you don't think you're good enough. I think you're an incredibly beautiful and resilient woman with a kind and gentle nature. You've handled on your own whatever life has given you. I have no doubt that you are exactly the one I'd be proud to have by my side."

Her eyes bore into mine, and I feel my resolve slip. I've worked hard to keep my distance from her, but holding her in my arms, I feel myself weakening. My gaze goes to her lips, and I'm helpless to stop myself from leaning into her space. Her tongue comes out and wets her lips, and my cock twitches. Just one taste. Then a miracle happens. She puts her hands on my chest and leans closer, until we are no more than a breath apart. Her eyes fix on my mouth.

"Duke, what are we doing?" she asks, her voice just a husky whisper.

I caress her cheek and begin to harden when she closes her eyes and nuzzles my palm. "I don't know, but I'm tired of fighting it." I answer her honestly.

Her eyes open slowly. "Me, too," she says. I see her need, her desire. She wants this every bit as much as I do.

Her hands inch up my chest. Mine wrap around her narrow waist, and I press her into my chest. I've never had a woman look at me with such burning passion. "Harlow," I say right before my lips connect with hers.

My body responds by swelling as my mouth devours hers. I clutch her tighter, moving my hands to her hips, pressing her against my hardness. I angle my head, deepening the kiss; our tongues touch, caress, and I groan from craving her so badly. "I can't stop myself from wanting you. You make me want to touch you, kiss you, and taste you, everywhere."

"I could be on board with that." She's in my arms, and we're on our way to my bedroom before our next breath.

In my bedroom, I let her feet fall to the carpet. "I want to see you." Her face shyly flushes pink, and I tip her chin up with my finger. "You're beautiful, Harlow. Never be embarrassed to show your body to me. I will worship every inch of your skin before this night is over."

She takes a few steps away. Her chin rises proudly, and I watch, mesmerized, as she unzips her dress and lets it fall in a puddle at her feet. I have a difficult time catching my breath. She's perfection. "I need to taste you," I say as I fall to my knees before her. I can't physically wait another minute, another second.

CHAPTER TEN

Harlow

The burning look in Duke's eyes gives me the confidence to tease him in stripping my clothes from my body. I track Duke's movements as he lowers himself to his knees. My stomach warms from his lips, as they slowly press kisses to my chilled skin. My heart races from the anticipation of where his kisses may lead. I'm not inexperienced, but I've never experienced that. But with Duke, I crave it all.

"Harlow?" he asks, looking up into my eyes.

I glance down and can only nod. The sight of Duke below me, touching me, making me flush with need, makes my heart nearly beat out of my chest. His eyes tip upward, connect with mine, and hold me captive. His hands on the back of my legs slide smoothly toward the place where I so want him to be. "Duke…." My voice sounds strange to my ears, low and breathless. His wondering hands travel to cup my cheeks and his fingers slipped under the elastic of my underwear. I'm so glad I have something silky and sexy for him to remove.

My hands brace against his hard, warm shoulders as he slides my panties down my legs and tosses them to the floor. I squeeze my eyes shut. *Oh, my God. I'm standing in front of Duke, naked.* Bravely, I open one eye, and my stomach clenches when Duke's eyes are feasting on me…there. I gain courage from his reaction.

"Harlow," he says with awe.

I can't look away as he moves his head closer. My eye flutter closed as I await his touch.

"You're stunning, Harlow. Beautiful." His breath caresses my skin before he kisses my lower stomach.

Under his eyes, I do feel beautiful. Shivers run up my spine and pull deep inside me. Slowly, he lifts one foot and drapes my leg over his shoulder. I swallow my breath as I stare down into his eyes just before he disappears between my legs. My head falls back, and a tortured moan leaves my lips when his warm breath touches my inner thigh.

"Do you want me to kiss you here?" he asks.

The foot I was balancing on begins to wobble, my fingers dig into his muscles to keep myself upright. "Oh, please, yes!" I plead.

I tremble as his mouth closes over the quivering bud at

the very heart of me. Never have I been so aroused, needy, frantic for something that only Duke can give me. "Duke," I murmured, feeling completely stripped bare, vulnerable in ways I'd never been before.

Slowly, my eyes open, and I glance down. Duke's impeccably groomed hair is tousled and messy from my hands, a sight I'd never thought to witness. Of their own accord, my hands run through his dark locks, and I shame-lessly press him tighter against me. Duke groans.

Mesmerized, I watch the movement of his head as he makes my blood boil with his lips, tongue, even his teeth, nipping against the delicate skin between my legs. My fingers grip his hair tighter as pressure builds beneath his tongue. So quickly I'm close, and that's never happened before. "Duke, oh, oh…" There's nothing fake about what he's making me feel.

His breath wafts over my sensitive bud as he says, "Come for me, love."

Love. I shiver and would have fallen if his strong hands hadn't wrapped around my waist to keep me from sliding to the ground. Sounds leave my mouth. Were they even words or just mindless expressions? I can take no more and finally let the orgasm wash over my body, consuming me with an intensity that leaves me breathless. Duke holds me as I tremble through the rushing waves, cresting in pulses that eventually ebb into calmness until I'm scooped up and laid gently on the bed. He follows me down and lies beside me and says "Harlow, I've never had unprotected sex. I don't want anything preventing me from being as close to you as possible."

His eyes stare into mine as he gives me time to think and process. I know what he's asking. And I know that protection means casual sex. And trusting the other person with your safety means a relationship. Is he saying he wants more with me? Can I handle more? I remember what Kaylee said about giving this attraction between us a chance. I want that chance, so I smile up into his eyes and say, "I want that too, Duke, but it can't happen now."

His nods, understanding my meaning. His eyes dim, but without pause he reaches into the bedside table and quickly rolls on the condom. He leans down and brings our lips together as he enters me slowly. I feel stretched and full.

He must have felt me tense because he stops and asks, "Has it been a while?"

I nod shyly. It's been a few years, actually.

"Me too," he admits.

My gaze meets his, and we both smile. He couldn't have said anything more perfect. In only a few gentle thrusts, he has me once again climbing to reach the final peak that will plunge me over the top. He follows me over, and together we ride the crest to the most powerful orgasm of my life. I never knew it could feel this strong, this intense. He drops a kiss on my lips before rolling off the bed to take care of the condom. He returns to bed, tucks my head under his chin, and pulls me into his body as he caresses my back. I'm so relaxed and deliciously sated. My eyes droop, and I could easily fall asleep in his arms—until his next words make my eyes pop open.

"There's one more thing you should know. I also told my mum you were my girlfriend," Duke says.

I lean back to see his face. He's serious. "Girlfriend?" I ask.

He nods. "Yes," he answers, then kisses my forehead and tucks me back under his chin.

My hand rests on his chest. He can't be serious. Maybe we have different definitions. "As in pretending to be your girlfriend to get your mother off your back?" I ask, because that's the only reason I can come up with.

He pauses, and his hand caressing my back stops in mid-stroke. "Well, we could do that, or we could make it real."

I feel his lips drop a kiss to the top of my head, and my heart jumps into staccato speed. "I don't know if that's wise," I say quietly.

"Why not?" he asks.

This time I pause before answering. "Because you'll end up breaking my heart."

"I would rather cut out my own heart than hurt you. But you are right to be cautious. There are responsibilities in my life that prevent me from offering you more than what we have now."

"I know all about responsibilities, and I know what you

mean." I never let myself dream he'd ask me for more, because I couldn't survive when he leaves. "I'll go with you to the wedding," I say, and his lips take mine again. I may be making the biggest mistake of my life, but I'm giving us a chance.

CHAPTER ELEVEN

Duke

I take Harlow's hand after sliding into the car seat beside her. Whatever our relationship is, it's settled into a near-blissful life. My feelings for her over these weeks have grown to the point that I can never get enough of her. She sleeps in my bed, which I've begun to consider our bed, and I always want her. Even if I've worn her out with orgasms when we go to bed, I still reach for her several times during the night. And in the morning, our showers have become my favorite part of the day. She's mine. I only have to convince her of that.

The only thing that mars our idyllic life is that sometimes I feel like there's a brick wall between us. I can't help believing it has to do with her father.

We did work on her business plan, and her friends have had several work sessions to help her increase her inventory. They say they're working, but the amount of laughter and wine involved makes me question this. I'm happy to see how close she's become with her friends, though; I don't imagine she's had much of that in her life.

I still have one last admission to make. It could possibly be the straw that breaks the camel's back where our future together is concerned. I've come to realize that I need a future with her. And my time has run out. Once we arrive at the airport, she's going to know. I pull on the too-tight collar of my dress shirt, trying to get a bit more air to my lungs. If I can just get her in the air, she'll have no option but to listen.

She leans over and lays her hand on my arm. I cover it with mine. "When we get to England, will someone be waiting on us at the airport?" she asks, her eyes anxiously peering out the windows.

I laugh and pull her into my side. I like her there. "Yes, but I'm not sure who."

She nods then looks my way with apprehension visible in her eyes. "And you let your mom know what time we arrive?"

I kiss her temple and grin. "Come here." This time I pull her into my lap. "There's no need to be nervous."

Our gazes meet, and I want to calm all the worry I see in

hers. "You said your mother can be hard to get along with. What if she doesn't like me?" Her eyes are big and beautiful and trusting. I feel like a cad.

"I like you, and that's all that matters." I press a kiss to her lips, and I love how she molds herself into my body as I deepen the kiss. I run my fingers through her soft curls and hold her face in my hands as my lips explore and tease until I hear, "Duke. I need you."

That's the wanton sound I wanted to hear. "Jeffrey is up front only a few feet away. I'll give you want you want, but you have to be quiet." Her body shivers in unrestrained anticipation at the thought of being caught. My precious girl. My eyes connect with Jeffrey, and he quickly complies with my silent request and raises the partition between us. I crush my lips to hers and catch the sound of her whimper. I would never share our pleasure with anyone. My hand moves up her slender thigh, under her dress, and to the top of her leg, then my finger slips under the elastic of her panties. Her legs fall open, inviting me in.

I tease her with my touch in all the places that drive her crazy, except the one that will give her what she wants.

"Duke, please!" she whispers.

I slide my finger over her clit, rolling it between my thumb and forefinger. Her head falls back, breaking our kiss as her body begins to shake. Her nipples push through the silk of her blouse like hardened steel nubs.

"There. Right there," she groans.

I watch her face as I push a finger deep inside while

continuing to rub slow, gentle circles over her clit. The glow of her skin, the sublime need—she's fucking beautiful. I add a second finger; her eyes open and meet mine, begging me to take her over the top. How can I deny her request? Doing so would deny us both. I curve my fingers and find the bundle of nerves inside, pressing and gently rubbing until I feel the tensing sign of her impending release.

"That's it, love. Let go. I've got you." I stroke her only a few more times before she shatters in my arms. I watch in awe as she clamps down around my fingers and completely destroys me. I slow my movements to sync with the fading spasms. She slumps against me and takes a deep, shuddering breath as I slowly remove my fingers from her warm depths.

She looks up at me with drowsy devotion in her eyes.

"Duke…" she lets my name fall from her lips.

I know what she's trying to tell me, but I can't let her go on. Not until she knows the truth. "I know, love."

"I can't believe we did that," she whispers, and her cautious eyes move from mine to the darkened glass behind the driver, then quickly back to me. "You…"

I stop her with a finger to her swollen lips. "I will always take care of you, Harlow. I would never allow anyone to share what is ours alone. Your pleasure is for me only."

She smiles, and my cock swells to bursting when she says, "That's so hot."

I groan and drop my head onto hers. This little minx is

going to be the death of me. I don't want to leave the inside of the limousine. I want to stay inside with her forever. I hear Jeffrey's door open and close, and I know we have only a few more moments left inside our bubble. I help her straighten her skirt and drop a last kiss to her lips as the car door opens. Once I tell her the truth, will I ever experience what we just shared again? I can't honestly say, and that's something that chills me to the core.

"Duke, where are we?" She takes in the area, and her eyes come back to me.

"This is the area for private planes." I vaguely explain. I need her to be onboard before I tell her. With my hand on the small of her back, I steer her toward the stairs leading up to the plane.

Her eyes sparkle as she asks, "We're flying to England in a private plane?"

"Yes." I nod to the jet we're quickly approaching. "That's our ride. It belongs to my family."

"Oh," is all she says until we're about to walk up the stairs to enter the plane. She stops to point to the design painted on the side of the aircraft. "What does that mean?"

"That's the Ainsworth family crest," I explain, pressing my hand against her back, prompting her to climb the steps.

"Oh." Again, that's her only comment. But I can see her mind working to put the pieces together as we climb the stairs.

Once we enter, she stops, her eyes moving from the

front leather seats to the back couches and entertainment center.

"Good afternoon, Your Grace," the flight attendant greets us using my title, and my eyes lock on Harlow. Slowly she turns, and I see the question in her eyes.

"Hello, Marissa. We don't require anything at the moment. I'll ring if we do." Harlow's head tips, and her eyes fill with confusion. I know when she sees the guilt showing on my face, because her eyes darken with rage.

"Yes, Your Grace." I hear Marissa close and lock the outer door before moving to the front and closing the partition between, but my eyes are still on Harlow. Her back straightens, and I see that beautiful, stubborn chin lift.

The pilot comes on the speaker and requests we buckle for takeoff. In a daze, Harlow drops to the first leather seat she comes to. Her fingers fumble with the seatbelt, and I finally lean over and snap it into place for her. She cuts me with her stare. This time, I'm the first to look away.

We're airborne before I speak. "Harlow, I can explain."

"Now?" she snaps. "You want to explain now? Not when we met. Or when we…we…you know. But now?" she asks with a disappointed bite to her voice.

I reach to take her hand, but she instead clasps her hands together on her lap. I try not to let her rejection of my touch hurt, but it does. "My name is actually Oliver, and I'm the Duke of Ainsworth Hall."

Her gaze sweeps to mine, and she says, "Oliver." Her

lips threaten to tip, but then her eyes narrow, and she's right back to being angry.

I nod. "Yes. I never meant to…misinform you of my identity. When I first moved to Treemont, I did introduce myself as Duke Oliver Ainsworth. Everyone simply misinterpreted my title as my name. I didn't correct them, because I enjoyed not having all the pomp and circumstance that comes with an English title."

She crosses her legs, then her arms underneath her luscious breasts. "I see," she says as her foot starts to swing, a sure sign of her temper.

"Are you angry?" I ask, afraid of the answer.

She sighs and uncrosses her arms, then turns to look at me. "I don't know what I am. I guess I'm hurt most of all. I thought we… I trusted you, and that's something I don't do easily. What type of a relationship do we have if you don't trust me, either? What am I even talking about? You're a Duke. There is no relationship." The distress in her voice wounds me.

I could point out that she's still keeping things from me, but I don't think now is the appropriate time. "You're wrong, love. What I feel for you has never changed. I'm sorry, Harlow. I do trust you, and I have been honest with you. I know it was wrong to keep the truth from you, but I hope you can forgive me."

She sits back in the seat and is quiet for a few moments. I know she's working through things in her mind. I give her time to process. "I'm not up on titles and things like that, but isn't a Duke kind of like a prince?" she asks.

"Not a prince, but next in the line of peerage," I explain and cringe at the wide-eyed look she gives me.

Again, she pauses before asking. "So, does that mean you're related to the royal family?"

I knew this was coming, and I hate to crush the hopeful expression on her face. "Not all Dukes are directly related."

She nods and asks, "But some are?"

"Yes." My one-word answer does nothing to calm the rising panic I see forming in her eyes.

"And are you?" she asks, her voice barely above a whisper.

I can do nothing more than answer honestly. "Yes."

She looks down to the plush carpet beneath our feet. "Wait. The wedding we're going to. Who's getting married?"

"I told you, my cousin is getting married." I swallow hard. "My cousin the prince."

She snaps her seatbelt open, pushes to her feet, and begins to pace. "You are taking me to a royal wedding? One that has been talked about in every media outlet for over a year? The one that is going to be on national television?" Her hands gesture wildly with each word.

Several times I try to interject, but each time I open my mouth, she shushes me with a finger or a piercing gaze.

"There will be famous people there as well as kings and queens. Oprah is going to be there! I have no idea how to act. What will I say? Am I even supposed to say anything? Maybe I'm not allowed to talk. And what will I wear? I certainly can't wear what I brought. They'd take one look at me and escort me from the premises for improper attire. Our picture could be in the news. They'll probably wonder why the Duke of Ainsworth is accompanied by…me, when you could have had your pick of heiresses or princesses who are more suited. And you know what, Du—*Oliver*? They'd be right!"

Spent, she slumps into the seat beside me. "I think I'm going to be sick," she mumbles.

I bite my lips to keep from chuckling. "Are you finished now?" I ask, noticing she is a bit green.

"Probably not," she answers, rubbing her eyes.

I grin and pick her up, happy that she allows me to, and carry her to the couch, where I sit with her on my lap. I'm finding this to be a favored position. I kiss her lips, and my heart flutters at her response. Perhaps all is not lost. "Love, I will be with you every step of the way. And if our picture does make a media outlet, they will think I'm one lucky chap to have such a gorgeous woman on my arm. As far as clothes go, my mum will take care of everything."

Her frightened eyes shine up into mine. "Oh, Duke. I don't want to embarrass you. Maybe I should just stay at your house."

I brush her lips again, and she relaxes into my embrace. "I'll not even entertain that idea. In fact, I think you need a bit more convincing on exactly how delicious I think you are." My brow rises, and I know she gets my point.

Her mouth opens, and a puff of breath escapes. "Oh, really? I'm not sure I'm through being mad at you."

I pick her up and walk to the bedroom. "Okay, you just continue being mad, and let me make it up to you." I have a lot of loving to do before we hit England.

CHAPTER TWELVE

Harlow

I take another look at the castle and place my hand in Duke's. I don't think I will ever see him as Oliver. He helps me from the car and places his hand on my lower back. I feel his strength, and I'm probably going to need it. The massive double doors open, and a prim and proper gentleman in a dark-gray suit greets us. He looks just like Alfred Pennyworth from Batman. I hide my grin.

"Welcome home, Your Grace," he says in a very English accent.

It sounds strange to hear Duke addressed so formally. How many infractions of the English codes have I already trodden all over since I've known Duke? But then he was simply Duke—not *the* duke. And, frankly, I'm not sure how I feel about that. We've never talked about a future, and maybe that was intentional on his part. My gaze moves over the magnificence of the home before me. I suddenly feel very inadequate.

"Thank you, Billings. It's good to be back," Duke says.

"Her Grace is awaiting you in the white drawing room," Billings announces.

Duke seems completely unconcerned that his mother has been waiting. "Billings, this is Ms. Davidson. Would you please see her set up in the rose bedroom?"

"Ms. Davidson." Billings nods in greeting then asks, "In the family wing, sir?" At Duke's nod, Billings quickly adds, "Right away, Your Grace."

"What was that about?" I ask as we climb the curved staircase.

Duke leans in closer and whispers, "I want you close to me. I have nefarious plans for you later."

I gasp. "My panties are suddenly damp," I say with a devious grin.

Duke groans. "That wasn't nice."

I chuckle. "But true."

With a hand to my arm, Duke stops me on the landing. His hand goes to my cheek, and I lean into his touch. "I wish I could carry you straight to my room and bypass the meeting with my mum," he says.

I smile up at him. "Me too. But we need to get this over with."

We walk through the wooden doors, and I'm suddenly transported into another time, another era. My eyes go from the family crest inlaid in the marble-tiled floor to the crystal five-tiered chandelier, that has to be as tall as I am, hanging a good twelve feet above us. My gaze widens to take in the intricate, twelve-inch plaster molding with gold trim that runs the entire length of the room.

"You grew up here?" I ask as I slowly make a three-sixty turn. I can't see a little boy feeling very comfortable living in a museum.

"For the most part. When I wasn't away at boarding school."

What must it be like to live in such wealth? I finally pull my gaze away from the ceiling and move to the double staircase in front of us, which looks like arms opened to welcome us. I wonder if there is a going-up side and a going-down side. Like the doors of a diner I worked in once. It was so hard for me to remember to go in the right door to the kitchen and exit the kitchen using the opposite door. More than one tray of food had been dumped on the floor during my short stint as a waitress. I hadn't been lying when I'd told Kaylee I wasn't very good at that job.

Duke—*Oliver*—leads me past beautiful paintings, to a room underneath the stairs. Inside, an uncomfortable-looking couch and four high-back chairs were arranged around an impressive inlaid marble fireplace. A regal woman wearing a navy-blue fitted skirt and jacket, dark hair artfully arranged on top of her head, rises from a small writing desk near a floor-to-ceiling window to greet us.

"Mum, it's so good to see you," Duke says and give his mother a kiss on her cheek.

"Oliver. I take it your travels went well?" she says, her accent much heavier than Duke's.

He puts his hand on my lower back, and I'm thankful for the support. "Yes, ma'am. We arrived safely, as you can see."

I'm stunned at how formal they sound. Much more like acquaintances than a mother and son who haven't seen each other in months.

She turns her eyes toward me, and I almost cringe. "Are you going to introduce me to your...friend?" she asks.

I can feel her intense scrutiny. She frowns at my simple denim skirt and cotton blouse. I don't have any problem seeing her disapproval. I cut my eyes to Duke. He should have told me I needed to dress differently. Of course, it wasn't until we were miles high in the air that I discovered I was visiting royalty.

"Mum, may I introduce Ms. Harlow Davidson?"

Suddenly I don't know if I'm supposed to curtsy, kiss her hand, or shake it. I make a horrible attempt. "Hi. Nice to meet you, Mrs. Ainsworth."

"How do you do." She tilts her head back and looks down her nose at me.

I never knew that was an actual look. Mrs. Ainsworth has that look down pat. "I'm fine, thanks."

She gets a sour, condescending look on her face and says, "No, that is how you properly address someone. You say, 'How do you do?' And you may call me Lady Ainsworth."

"Mum..." Duke starts, but my hand on his arm halts his defense. This is my fight. My eyes narrow. *Oh, no, she didn't.* My spine straightens, but I smile graciously and politely say, "Oh, excuse me, Lady Ainsworth. I thought when greeting a guest in your home, you made them feel welcome."

Duke turns a chuckle into a cough. "Mum," Duke cautions.

We both cut our gaze to Duke. When we're once again in our face-off positions, I think I may see just a tiny smidge of respect in her eyes. "Please, won't you have a seat?" she says, not waiting for us to join her.

I sit on the couch and find I was correct; it is horribly uncomfortable. I can't imagine curling up with a good book on any surface in this entire room. I drop my bag to the floor and pick it right back up and place it beside me on the couch when Lady Ainsworth frowns. Again.

"Perhaps your...friend would like to freshen up from her trip while we chat," she smiles politely.

She said the word *friend* like she'd say, 'I have dog poop on my shoe.' "That sounds like a good idea," I reply quickly. Escape is an excellent idea. "I could use some freshening."

Without a sound, Billings appears in the doorway.

Duke's gaze meets mine, and I nod, letting him know I'm perfectly fine with leaving.

"If you will go with Billings, he'll show you to the yellow room," Lady Ainsworth says.

Duke interrupts, "I've had Billings put Harlow in the rose room."

"Oliver." The disapproval of the new room assignment is clear to see and hear.

Dukes eyes narrow on his mother. "Mum. The rose room."

After a silent battle, she nods. "Fine. Billings, the rose room."

Duke gives my hand a squeeze and I skedaddle before she can change her mind. I'm in the beautiful rose-pink bedroom before I remember I left my bag on the couch and that I'd promised to call Kaylee when we arrived. I run back downstairs, hoping I can remember how to find the rose room again. As I near the drawing room, I hear Lady Ainsworth speaking.

"Oliver, I so had my hopes up when you told me you were seeing someone. But, dear, she simply won't do. What were you thinking to bring that woman to your cousin's wedding? She'll have no idea how to act."

"Mum, I invited her because I want her here. She's my friend," he says sternly.

"Oh, please. I was your father's wife for over thirty years. He had many *friends*, but he never invited them into our home."

My hand covers my mouth to keep from gasping out loud. Duke's father had affairs? Wait. Did she just call me a...

"Mum. My relationship with Harlow is none of your business."

"Fine. She can be your paramour, but take Celeste to the wedding, since you won't consider Alyssa. We can ship Ms. Davidson off on some touristy thing. Send her to Paris for the week."

"Mum, Harlow is going to attend Jamie's wedding. With me. I've already told you neither Celeste nor Alyssa will be my date."

"She doesn't even know how to dress appropriately or have proper decorum. The event is going to be televised. We will be a world-wide laughingstock."

"I'm sure you can have her dressed appropriately before the first event."

"Oliver, at this late date, I'm sure Mr. Ransome is booked solid. It's impossible."

"Mum, you need to make an effort to accept Harlow."

She gasps, and I can just see her inflate. "What are you saying, Oliver?"

"You know exactly what I'm saying."

I don't. I don't have a clue what he means.

"It will never work, you know. She'd never survive in our world."

For a long time, I hear nothing, then I hear her sigh. "I'll do what I can. I shudder to think what will happen if we have to pick off-the-shelf outfits for someone her size."

My size? I look down at my size-six skirt. What's wrong with my size?

"Thank you, Mum."

I turn to sneak away, but I pause when I hear Lady Ainsworth's next words.

"Oliver, you know how unsuitable she is to be the Duchess of Ainsworth."

I hold my breath to hear Duke's answer.

"I know my duty, Mum. Who I decide to marry is not up for debate," he says.

I feel an ache in the region of my heart, but I'm not sure why. I never anticipated a proposal from Duke, but even I know how impossible that sounds.

"Oliver, need I remind you that your time to return is growing closer? You need heirs, and you aren't getting any younger. Celeste is perfect for you. She has breeding and a good family name."

"I'm going upstairs now, Mum. We'll see you for dinner."

"At seven, sharp, mind you. You know how much I detest tardiness."

I don't wait around to hear more. I run up the stairs, forgetting all about my purse. I go straight to the en-suite bathroom and lock the door. I have no idea if Duke will come to my bedroom, but I need time to process what I've just overheard.

So many thoughts are running around in my head. The most important one being, *Why did Duke bring me?* He had to have known his mother wouldn't like me. Am I his amusement while he's here? A way to soften the meanness of his mother? Or a way to irritate her more? Maybe I'm his comic relief for the duration of the wedding festivities. He had to know I'd fit in about as well as a lobster in a pot factory. What did she mean about him returning? Duke hasn't said anything about returning to England for good.

"Harlow?" Duke asks from the other side of the bathroom door.

I close my eyes. I'm not ready to talk to him. "Yes?" I try to answer normally.

"Are you all right? You sound strange." I hear the concern in his voice.

I look in the mirror and force a smile before saying, "Of course. I'm fine. Did you want something?"

He pauses, and I'm afraid he's going to insist I open the door, but then he says, "Yes. I'll meet you in the hallway at 6:45 for dinner. Please dress accordingly."

With the fake smile on my face, I answer, "Okay. Great. I'll be ready." I press my ear to the door and listen for my bedroom door to close. When I hear it click, I peek and find the coast clear. I fall back on my bed and groan. When did my life become so complicated?

I look for my suitcase and find it in the closet. Everything I'd packed is already hanging in the massive walk-in. I take down a pretty blue dress that was part of my fairytale closet and hold it up, checking myself out in the floor-length mirror. For a moment, I wonder if it's too late to ask Duke to send me back home.

The antique clock on the side table shows my time is quickly running out. I certainly don't want to be late. I jump into action, rushing to dress and apply a little bit of makeup. I even take time to put my hair up into a bun on top of my head, pinning it in place with several bobby pins that I find in the bottom of my makeup bag. I'm pleased with my reflection in the mirror, but I don't look familiar. The soft fabric slides over my waist and hips, hitting me mid-thigh. I slip on black heels and immediately feel myself toppling. I take a few laps around my bedroom, trying to feel comfortable being four inches taller. I decide it's never going to happen.

A knock at my bedroom door sends me tottering to answer it. I open the door to a much different Duke than I've ever seen. The suit he's changed into is in a class all its own. I have no trouble imagining him as a man of position and wealth.

"You're beautiful, Harlow," he says, touching my cheek with his finger. My skin tingles under his touch.

I brush my hands down the fabric of my dress, making sure there are no wrinkles. "Thank you. You're rather dashing yourself."

Before I can stop him, he pulls the pins from my hair.

"Duke! What are you doing?" I run to the bathroom, stabbing my head in the process of putting my hair back up.

He comes up behind me and lays his hands on my shoulders. "Leave it down." I look up and see him in the mirror. "Harlow, I want to apologize for my mother's behavior. I'm sorry she made you feel unwelcome. This is my home, and you are my guest. My mum knows this, but she has a hard time letting go. I want you here, and I'll make sure your visit is memorable. I wouldn't blame you for going back to the States, but I hope you'll stay."

What could I say? I turn in his arms and wrap my arms around his neck. His eyes look into mine. "I'll stay. But I can't promise to hold my tongue if Cruella starts something."

The corners of his eyes crinkle in laughter. "I would expect my fierce warrior to do nothing less."

Later that night, I lie in Duke's bed and stare at the ceiling, thinking about our dinner with his mom. The food had been heavy and creamy. Not really to my liking, but Duke seemed to enjoy it. Who am I to complain? A few short months ago, I was surviving on very little food. I'm proud of myself for not putting his mom in her place. I was tempted several times, but I was determined to be the better person, even if she didn't realize that phenomenal feat. Duke, however, had put an early end to our evening by refusing dessert, which had been the only thing I'd been looking forward to. He'd left me in the hallway outside our rooms to attend to an errand. I'm not sure what he did, but I have my suspicions. Less than an hour later, he'd walked into my bedroom, carried me from my bed, tossed me into his, and then spent plenty of time making sweet love to erase the horrendous evening we'd spent with his mother while she made polite but snide remarks about me all through dinner. I'm still confused about what she said about his time running out, and maybe even a bit hurt that Duke has never mentioned anything about his return.

Three days later, I find myself at a formal dinner party in honor of the wedding couple, thankful that I'm not in a dress that makes me cringe. Trying to please Duke's mother, I met with her designer and bit my tongue as they talked about me while I was two feet away from them. And I'm *not* hippy. The dress they'd made for me to wear tonight was the color of dirt and fit me like a potato sack. I could have made something nicer with my Designer Suzy Sewing Machine when I was ten. But I've never attended royal parties, so I said nothing. Duke's face when he opened my bedroom door tonight told me all I needed to know. It's a horrific dress.

His face had pinched in anger, then he turned on his heel and marched down the hallway. I have no idea where he went, but he came back in less than five minutes with a beautiful jewel-toned green gown. I didn't ask where he got it, and I didn't want to know because I was afraid it's was his mom's. It was a bit small in the chest and the length was about two inches too long, even with my heels, but it was one hundred percent better than the dirt dress.

Nervously, I glance around our table, feeling confident as I'm dressed similarly to everyone else. I was happy to see we were not sitting at the royal table with the prince and his bride. I didn't need the added pressure. But I must admit, the estate where the party is being held is glamorous. I could have been transported into a lavish movie set. I've never seen so many jewels and silks and satins in one place. We'd had pre-dinner drinks, where I'd met the prince and his bride. I even managed a passing curtsey. Ms. Ainsworth —rather, *Lady* Ainsworth—had been completely charming. But I don't believe her opinion of me has changed.

I take a breath to ease my racing heart as I stare at my place setting. There are so many forks and spoons and dishes in front of me, and I feel every eye in the room focused on me. I reach for my water glass, splattering a small drop of water on the linen tablecloth from my trembling. Duke's hand covers mine, and I'm instantly grounded. I smile at him in gratitude.

"You're beautiful, Harlow, and you belong here just as much as anyone else in this room."

My face is frozen into a polite smile. He always knows what I'm thinking. But he's wrong. No, I don't. Can't he see that? I don't belong here, and I never will. A woman to my right, wearing an incredibly silly-looking thing on the side of her head, looks at me and glares. I glare back, refusing to allow her to see how her disapproval hurts. I know all about mean girls, and I learned you can't show fear. They feed on your insecurities.

"Don't," Duke whispers.

"I'm not like these people," I answer just as quietly. God, please tell me I'm nothing like them.

"And, for that, I'm eternally thankful," he says as he nudges my arm and nods at the awful woman. "That's Mrs. Earntswhile. At least, that's her current name. She's been married five times. Her first husband caught her having a lay-about with the gardener. There's still speculation as to the parentage of her first-born son. Her second husband had a horrible problem betting on the horses and lost most of their fortune. When he could no longer support her in the style she expected, she divorced him. Husband number three spent more time in Paris than he did at home. Eventually he divorced her to marry the mother of his three children. The ones he'd been keeping secret in Paris. I'm not sure about husband number four, but I believe Mum said it only lasted a few years. Now this chap is husband number five."

My eyes move to the sad-looking man beside her. He wasn't engaging in any of the conversation around him. Instead, he was moving the food around on his plate while being ignored by his wife. The rich certainly had their own set of problems. I feel sorry for Mr. Earntswhile.

With a sigh, I pick up one of the three forks beside my plate and stab something green. I have no idea what I'm eating. It seems the more expensive the food is, the less it resembles its true form. Even after swallowing, I'm still not sure what I've eaten.

"I don't know what any of this food is," I whisper.

He chuckles and wipes his mouth with his linen napkin. "And you think I do? As long as it's expensive and can be bragged about to supposed friends, that's all the English care about." Duke winks and takes a bite of what I think may be Brussels sprouts. I've just never seen purple ones before.

I smile, and some of the butterflies in my stomach settle. Then I admit, "I'm afraid I'm going to make a complete mess of things and embarrass you."

Duke frowns and opens his mouth to answer, just as someone taps him on the opposite arm. The gentleman escorting Mrs. Ainsworth sitting across from me chuckles, and my eyes dart to his. He'd been introduced as Mr. Compton.

"I wish you would make a mess of things." Mr. Compton says with a wicked grin. "It would be the most excitement had by the upper echelon of the English society in at least a decade." He grins, drains his wine glass, then holds it up in the air. A waiter rushes to refill the goblet. And Mr. Compton's eyes never left mine.

"It's not polite to listen in on others' conversations," I say with a raised brow, feeling uneasy.

He makes a grand show of dabbing each corner of his mouth with his napkin before answering. "Darling, don't you know the English are far from polite? Don't let them intimidate you. That's how they get their grins and giggles."

"Excuse me, Harlow," Duke leans over and says. "I have a call from the States I must take. Will you be all right while I'm gone?"

I want to say no, but instead I smile and reassure him, "Of course. I hope nothing is wrong."

He squeezes my hand. "I'll only be a moment."

When Duke leaves the room, it seems as if everyone considers me free game. The questions come fast and hard, and Mr. Compton smiles and takes it all in.

"Tell us, Ms. Davidson, what business are your family in?" I believe Mrs. Bentley is the name of the lady who asked.

"Um, well..." Saying my father is a gambling addict and I'm currently homeless and working in a tea bar wouldn't be appropriate. "Retail, ma'am."

Her nose turned up even more if that's possible.

"Really, what type?" another perfectly dressed lady asks.

My eyes move to her and I answer. "Tea, ma'am. I work at a tea shop."

"You own a tea shop? How quaint. An American with a tea shop!" A gentleman I have not been introduced to laughs at his own silly joke.

"No, sir. I don't own it. I work there." The entire table falls quiet.

"You're a laborer, then?" A lady from the end of the table asks as if the word sticks in her mouth.

I catch Lady Ainsworth's pleased eyes as I answer. "If you mean I serve tea to customers, then yes." I see linen napkins move over snickering mouths, and I want to crawl under the table. Instead, I sit up straighter and pierce them with my eyes.

"How did you and Oliver meet?" Ms. Bently asks.

My food is now forgotten. Even if I tried to choke down another bite, I'm sure it wouldn't go down without a fight. "In the tea shop. I fixed him a cup of tea and he tossed it in the trash." I smile to myself at the memory.

"The trash?" Another gentleman asks.

The lady beside him leans over and stage whispers, "Rubbish, dear. Trash is what Americans call rubbish."

I glance around the table, and every man, including Mrs. Ainsworth's escort, has a patronizing look on his face. They've already decided why they think Duke is associating with someone so far beneath his class. I feel the room closing in, and I can't breathe. I slide back in my chair, and it makes a screeching noise on the marble tile. All eyes in the room turn to me, even at the prince's table.

I stand up and toss my napkin in my plate. My face is flaming hot and my hands are shaking so badly I clench them at my sides and say, "If you'll excuse me. I, um, need to use the ladies' room."

I hear gasps behind me as I walk as fast as I can from the room. I suppose it's inappropriate to talk about using the bathroom, too. Once I'm clear of the doorway, I sprint down the hallway, searching for someplace to hide. "I don't belong here. I don't belong here," I say over and over to myself.

Finally, I squeeze into a niche that looks like a place used for clandestine affairs long ago. In actuality, it probably once housed a large plant or statue of some type. All I care about is that I fit, and nobody can find me. Just for a few moments.

The tap of heels on the marble floor coming closer to my hiding place sends me edging backward. Then I hear voices.

"Althea, stop. What do you hope to accomplish by confronting her?"

I shrink back even farther into the recess when I realize it's Lady Ainsworth and Mr. Compton.

"I intend to put a stop to this nonsense now. His whore just made a mockery of our family, and I will not let that happen again."

"Your son brought her as his guest. You should remember that."

"I can't stand by and let her humiliate us like she just did. She's a commoner sitting among royalty."

"If you confront her, you will be driving your son away, back to America. I thought your goal was to get him back to England and producing heirs. He's still young, Althea. She's a novelty to him. That's all. Let him fuck her and get her out of his system before he must come home and resume his duties. He's a smart man. He knows exactly what she is. Give him his freedom and let him have his little infatuation."

"But what if that takes years?"

"Don't be absurd. He's only fascinated with her because she's different. Their association will die out once he realizes she's only a sweet piece of ass with no substance. Let the boy have his whore for now, then he'll be ready to settle down. If memory serves, he has very little time left anyway."

"And what if she tricks him into getting her pregnant?" The bite in her voice is chilling.

"Then it will be dealt with. It's not like there aren't enough illegitimate heirs running around." He chuckles, and the wicked sound causes shivers to run down my spine.

"What do you expect me to do, pretend that she's one of us and belongs by his side?"

"I expect you to go back in there and say you regret Ms. Davidson is feeling unwell and will not be rejoining us."

"Fine."

"Don't worry, dear. He'll learn to keep his paramours separate from his responsibilities. Just like his mother and father did."

She gasps, and I peer around the corner to see them locked in an embrace, Mr. Compton devouring her lips in a very passionate kiss. Then I hear the hurried tapping of her heels going back to the dining room.

I try to slow my breathing while I wait for Mr. Compton

to leave, but instead I hear the clipped sounds of his shoes coming closer.

"Were you able to get all that, dear?" Mr. Compton says with a sneer. I press myself back into the wall when he touches me with his fingers and trails a path down my cheek and neck, stopping as he nears my chest.

"While I do appreciate Oliver's taste in women, I'm afraid you just won't do. Perhaps you're feeling unwell and you must rush home?" The sneer on his face turns into a disgusting leer and makes me feel exposed and dirty.

"The rear entrance is that way." He points down a hallway. "Tell one of the drivers to take you back to Ainsworth Hall. Go ahead, fuck Oliver all you want. Your time is running out."

"What do you mean, running out?" I finally find my voice and ask.

"Oliver was given ten years to play his games in America before coming home to settle down and take on his responsibilities as Duke. By my calculations, he has only a few more months left."

I watch his back as he retreats, leaving me shivering, my back against the wall—in more ways than one.

CHAPTER THIRTEEN

Duke

I find her in her bedroom, sitting in the window seat, staring off into the dark night. When Mother said Harlow wasn't feeling well and went back to Ainsworth Hall, I immediately knew something wasn't right, especially when no one in the dining room would meet my eyes. This visit is turning out nothing like I'd hoped. How can I convince Harlow that a life with me would be a good thing if everyone continually tries to alienate her?

Her head slowly turns toward me when she hears me enter. She's been crying. Anger boils in my chest. What did they do? I work to calm myself before I ask, "Love, are you all right?"

She nods and gives me a small, weepy smile. "I'm sorry I left the way I did. I had a sudden headache."

Even though she does have a pinched look around her eyes, I don't think she's telling me the truth. "Harlow, what happened?"

She sighs and turns back to the window. "Why did you invite me here, Duke?"

She looks so lost. I want to go to her, but I don't. "What?"

She turns around on the window seat and asks, "Whatever this is between us, is it only about sex?"

This time I don't wait. Her question irritates me. I kneel and take her hands in mine. "I may have been dishonest with my position, but everything I've ever said to you or felt for you is truthful. I invited you here because I wanted to be here with you."

She nods like she understands what I'm saying then looks at our joined hands. "You're not just interested in me because I'm different than anyone you've ever known?"

I rest my forehead on her hands, kiss each one and then gaze into her eyes. "Why can't I find you irresistible because I do find you different?" I ask. I can see she wants to believe me, but something is holding her back.

"Your mom made it pretty clear I'm not welcome here. This is your cousin's wedding. I don't want to cause any problems."

I knew something happened tonight. I'm sure my mum is directly in the middle of whatever has put these doubts in

Harlow's mind. "My mother hasn't made my decisions since I was twelve and left home for boarding school."

"That may be, but I can't see myself ever fitting into this world, and I can't help thinking th-that…" She stumbles and stops, her eyes fill with tears, and it's my undoing.

I fight back. She has to see how good we are together, so I finish her sentence with a harshness I don't feel. "That I'm using you for sex. Because we both know how phenomenal our chemistry is. There can't be any other reason, can there?"

I watch her chin notch a few inches higher. The fire and spirt of this woman astound me. How can she question what I feel for her? "It's not just about sex. It's the way I feel when I'm with you. Each moment we're together is the best part of my day. Before you, my every thought was of business, mergers, acquisitions. Now I can't keep my mind focused on any other things because you fill me up completely. You make me smile, and you make me stop and find joy in life. I don't think I've ever found anything in my world to laugh about. But with you, I found my happiness. You, Harlow. You're my contentment."

I pull her tighter against my chest and rest my cheek on her bent head. "I've wanted you since the day you made me that horrid cup of tea. I took one look and knew you were someone I wanted to get to know. I never cared who you were or what you did. I wanted you. I want more with you." Just saying the words makes me realize how much I mean them.

I tip her chin up and gaze into her eyes. "Stay with me, Harlow. Let me show you that my world is better because you're in it. I don't care what anyone else says. Stay for me. For…us."

I swipe away the tears falling down her cheeks. "I don't know if I'm strong enough," she whispers.

I chuckle and clear the hair from her beautiful face. "Harlow, you are by far the strongest woman I've ever known. Tell me what happened tonight."

She sighs and stares at my shirt front. "After you left to take your call, some of the people at our table started asking catty questions, I'm sure to put me in my place."

"Harlow…"

She looks up, and I see the hurt in her eyes. It slays me. "Truly, they didn't bother me. I've dealt with ignorant people before. I stepped out of the room just to catch my breath, and I overheard a conversation between your mother and Mr. Compton. He implied your infatuation would run its course."

The wounded look on her face leads me to think there was much more said. "And you believed this?" I ask, my temper rising.

She shakes her head, and her eyes soften. "No. Not really. I mean, I know what he said was an attempt to put distance between us. No one was happy I was there, once they found out I work for a living."

"I was ecstatic you were there," I say, and see a smile pulling at the corners of her mouth. "Don't let them win,

Harlow. Believe in what we have, what we feel for each other."

She puts her cheek back on my chest. "I want to, Duke. I really do. But sometimes it's hard. In Treemont, it's easier to just be Duke and Harlow. I like that couple."

"I do too, love. But whether here or there, we're the same people, just with different circumstances. I think we are strong enough to get through both together."

She can't leave me. I press a kiss to the top of her head. Her nipples go hard and press against my chest. I want her just as I always do, but I think it's important that she understands my feelings are true with or without the pleasure we can bring to each other. I remove my clothes, dropping them where they fall. Then, with care, I quickly have her standing naked and glowing in front of me.

The passionate need in her eyes sends a stroke of hot desire straight to my hardened cock. There is no question that I desire her. But tonight is a night for healing and trusting. I pick her up and carry her to the bed, laying her gently in the middle before following her down, covering her, soaking her into every pore of my body.

"You're so beautiful," I say just before claiming her lips with mine. I then roll over and flip the switch that sends us into darkness. "Goodnight, love." I say and pull her into my arms. Her frustrated sigh brings a smile to my face. Then my eyes narrow, and my lips thin when I think about what she went through tonight. Tomorrow I'm going to have a long talk with Mum, and as far as Mr. Compton goes, I think it's time I assert my legal authority where he's concerned. He helped Mum through Father's passing, and he's kept things running while I've been in the States, but it's time to have a discussion about his place in my family. I will not allow him to put such doubts in Harlow's mind, even if he is close with my mum. Just *how* close, I shudder to think.

The next morning, I wake with Harlow's legs tangled in mine and all the covers on her side. I grin. I've never been so happy to wake up with a chill. I've known she's a cover hog for a while now, and I'm okay with that.

Her hand rests on my chest, and I cover it with mine. I've lain awake most of the night trying to decide how to go forward. Today I plan to keep Harlow to myself and show her a part of my home that I love. It's important that I make up for all the unpleasantness she's had to endure as my guest. With a little ingenuity and flexibility, I slide out of bed, throw on some clothes, and quietly slip out to put my plans in place. In record time, I return with a breakfast tray in hand to find her just waking up.

"Good morning, love." Her hair is tousled and wild, and my cock jerks. My eyes go to the vacant spot beside her and I reprimand myself for leaving my bed in the first place. But that wouldn't be what I hope to accomplish today. I keep walking past the bed and set my tray of goodies on a small table by the windows.

"I like it when you call me that." She gives me a sleepy smile and stretches, causing the sheet to slip, exposing the top curve of her breasts.

Each beat of my heart pulses through the lower part of my body. "Good to know."

Her cute little nose crinkles as she sniffs the air. "Is that cocoa I smell?"

I pick up a mug and carefully carry it to her. "And not just any cocoa, either. This is made from the best chocolate in the world. At least in my opinion. Our chef orders it from a chocolatier in France."

"But is it better than Hershey's?" Harlow asks.

My brow rises in confusion. "I'm afraid I don't know that one. You'll have to be the judge." I hand her the mug, and she purses her lips to blow across the top to cool the steaming liquid. My eyes stick on her lips, and my cock twitches. I want to lay her back down on the bed and have my wicked way with her, but that's not in the plan today. Today is all about Harlow.

She takes a sip and swallows. "It's delicious." She licks the whipped cream from her lips. I close my eyes and silently groan.

I turn away from the tempting sight and walk stiffly back to the tray. "I told you. And we also have a chocolate croissant."

Her eyes go large like a child in a candy store. "Oh my! I've never had one of those. It looks too good to eat."

I chuckle when her words are quickly followed by taking a huge bite. She closes her eyes, and the sounds coming from her mouth take me back to the sounds she makes when I've driven her wild with need. Rushing to the door, I call over my shoulder, "Enjoy your breakfast, then you can shower. I've left your clothes for the day in the bathroom. I'll meet you downstairs in thirty minutes. We have a big day planned."

I hear her laughter as I click the door closed. The little minx knew exactly what she was doing to me. My own grin turns into laughter as I walk down the ancient hallway to finalize our outing.

Exactly thirty minutes later, I hear her footsteps on the stairs. My mouth goes dry as my eyes follow her movements, and I wonder at my sanity for choosing her current outfit. The blue denim jeans fit her like a second skin, and the white tank top I'd chosen stretches across her breasts, accenting their lush fullness.

"I did wonder if you'd forgotten a particular piece of clothing, but from your reaction, I believe it was intentional," she says and my head jerks up to find a teasing sparkle in her eyes.

I shrug and try to hide my smile. "I can assure you I forgot nothing."

She rolls her eyes, and I can't help pulling her in for a brief kiss. "Come. We don't want to be late." I say, taking her hand.

"Where are we going?" she asks as we step outside and head toward the stables.

"It's a surprise."

She gives a squeal and hugs my arm to her breasts. "I like surprises."

"I know, love." I glance her way, and I'm stunned by her glowing face. This is the Harlow I know. I feel very remiss that I've not had her comfort and happiness foremost in my actions and thoughts.

As we near the barn, her steps slow. "Duke, what's that?" she asks cautiously.

I chuckle. "That's our transportation."

She shakes her head and pulls backward on my hand, away from our mounts. "But I don't ride. I've never been on a horse before. I've never even seen a horse in person."

I throw my head back and laugh. I take her hand and lead her to the sorrel. "This is Lucy, and she'll be your mount. She's very gentle and has an easy gate." I scratch the bay behind his ears. "And this gentleman is Major. He's a bit more spirited." The top of Harlow's head doesn't even reach the top of the saddle. She looks so small beside Lucy, and that makes me doubt my plans. "Would you rather ride with me?" I ask.

She bites her lips, but I can tell she's tempted. "You're sure she's gentle?"

I would never put her in danger. "When children visit, Lucy is their mount." I say, and wait for her to work through her nerves. I know she'll enjoy our ride, but we'll do whatever she decides.

She takes a step closer to Lucy, with her hand still firmly grasping mine. "I'm scared, but I really want to try."

I kiss her temple and smile. "We'll go slow, and I'll be beside you the entire time."

It only takes a brief introduction between the two, a basic riding lesson, and we're set to wander through the fields around the estate. I'm so proud and amazed by Harlow's strength and sense of adventure. She and Lucy have gotten along so well she even wanted to try a trot. That was when I regretted not selecting a bra to go with her outfit. I adjust in the saddle, and it's my own bloody fault.

I nod to the pond just visible in the distance. "Why don't we stop there and take a break?"

She scans the area and nods. "That sounds good. I never knew riding was so much fun."

The carefree look on her face makes me happy. "I'm glad you're enjoying it."

"Is that the pond your family used to picnic by?" she asks as we plod along.

I'm surprised she remembers our conversation from so long ago. I shouldn't be, though; Harlow has an uncanny ability to listen and store information away. "It is. I have an activity planned."

Her eyebrows waggle, and she says, "Really?" in a mocking voice.

"You wound me, Harlow. I told you this was a day for surprises, and I will not let you take advantage of me." I fake a dramatic pout, which makes her laugh.

"If you say so," she says, but she doesn't sound like she believes me.

I dismount and help Harlow down, steadying her when her feet touch the ground. She leans into me, and her breasts touch my chest. I hiss as if I've been burned. "You are a cruel woman, Ms. Davidson," I say, brow arched. She gives me an innocent grin in response. I take her hand and start walking toward the pond.

"This is lovely, Duke."

"I loved picnics here. It was one of the few times we got to relax together as a family. There were no itchy dress shirts or shoes that pinched. I didn't have to mind my manners and be the studious son and future duke. Here, I could just be a boy with his mum and dad."

"It sounds wonderful. Was it difficult growing up with so many responsibilities at such a young age?"

"Going off to school helped. I met good friends there. I wish you could meet them, but maybe next time. Rocco lives in Italy. He was the first friend I made at school when we both found ourselves dumped in the school's fountain by some older boys."

She gasps, and her expression turns livid in my defense. "That's horrible!"

I laugh and pull her in for a hug. "Oh, don't worry. We retaliated by sneaking ants into their beds." Harlow laughs, and the sound of her voice makes me smile.

"Bran and Luca are brothers and were my suite mates. They live in the Netherlands. As twins, they couldn't have been more different, but when they dressed alike, you couldn't tell them apart. A fact that we may have used to our advantage a time or two."

Her eyes shine as her brow tips upward. "It sounds like there may have been a girl or two involved."

She makes me laugh again. "And you would be correct. But a gentleman never tells. Jibri may be at the wedding. You'll like him. He lives in a palace in the middle of an animal sanctuary. It isn't unusual to find giraffes gazing at you through your bedroom window. Jibri does a lot of conservation and humanitarian work for his country."

"He sounds a lot like you."

"Perhaps. Come. Here is your first surprise." I wait for her to take in the remote-controlled boats waiting for us on the dock.

"Boats!" Harlow drops my hand and runs ahead like a little child at Christmas. I toss my head back and laugh.

After our boating excursion, we mount back up and ride to the ruins of a medieval castle, where our lunch is waiting. Then we ride into the village, where my stable master is waiting to trailer our mounts back home. We walk among

177

the art shops, visiting whichever ones catch our eyes. We have dinner at my favorite pub. Harlow orders fish and chips, disappointed when she discovers chips are nothing more than fries. After dinner, she wins two out of three games of darts then falls asleep on my shoulder as we drive back to the hall.

To me, our day was perfect. I wouldn't mind a lifetime of the same.

Harlow is my priority, and it takes me until later that night to figure it out, but I know what I have to do.

CHAPTER FOURTEEN

Harlow

The next morning, I wake to find Duke dressed and sitting on a chair near the window. I'm confused when I notice our suitcases sitting by the door. "Duke?" My brows draw together in question.

He stops reading his phone and looks my way with a smile. "Good morning, love."

"What's going on?" I ask and scoot up in the bed, leaning against the headboard.

He puts his phone down on the table and comes to sit on the bed and pulls me in for a kiss. "We're going home," he answers.

"Why? The wedding…" I stammer, unable to imagine

why he'd want to leave. Did I do something? Has he finally realized I don't belong here?

His eyes narrow in to focus on mine. "Stop. You did nothing wrong. We're leaving because I no longer want to be here. I've called my cousin and explained we're needed back home in the States."

There has to be more that he's not saying. I look up into his eyes and ask, "You're doing this for me?"

He takes my hands. "I'm doing this for *us*. If you're not happy, then I'm not either. I'm sorry I misjudged my family and so-called friends and put you in their line of fire."

My eyes soften, and I caress his cheek. "Don't, Duke. You can't take their issues on yourself. I don't want to run back home because they hurt my feelings. I want to stay and show them they weren't successful in tearing us apart."

He pulls me in for another kiss then smiles. "My fierce warrior. I know you would do just that. But I'm ready to go."

I stand back as Duke kisses his mom on the cheek and says goodbye. She's been giving me heated glances ever since she found out at breakfast that we were leaving early. I know she blames me, even though Duke explained it was his decision to leave. I have mixed feelings about our trip to England being over. The highlight is, by far, the day Duke and I spent together. I'll cherish those memories of just the two of us forever. I got to see a part of Duke that not many people know exist. But I still have one more thing I must do.

I squeeze Duke's hand and ask. "Can you wait for me in the car?"

He gives me a confused look but then nods and gives his mom a final goodbye.

I wait for him to get into the limousine before I turn my back to him and lower my voice so only Lady Ainsworth can hear. I can't leave without doing whatever I can for his future happiness. I see the love they both have for each other, and I can't believe his mother would want anything less. I meet her gaze and refuse to let her glaring look intimidate me.

"I realize this is the last time I will ever see you, but I wanted you to know that my feelings for Oliver were never about his position or his wealth. I care for your son. So much so that I want only his happiness. I'll be with Duke for as long as he wants me, but when we're over, I hope you will respect his decision for his future Duchess and not foist your selection on him."

I say what I'd been practicing, turn without waiting for her response, and join Duke in the car. I don't even look back as we pass through the gates. He doesn't question what I said to his mother. I would have told him if he had asked. Instead, he takes my hand and kisses the pulse point at my wrist.

"Are you sad to be leaving England?" I ask, hoping the

answer is similar to mine. It would suit me just fine never to step foot on English soil again.

He rubs his thumb in a caress over the spot he'd just kissed. I've come to love his touches.

He looks out the window at the passing scenery before answering. "England will always be my home. Eventually, I'll once again need to reside at Ainsworth Hall, but for now, I'm ready to return to Treemont."

I notice he doesn't say anything about his time in America running out, and that hurts. "Is it because you'll have responsibilities with your title?" I ask, giving him a lead in if he wants it.

"I'll want my children to be raised in the family home," he says.

The thought of Duke's children takes my breath. I've accepted that I won't be their mother. Besides, nothing since we landed over a week ago has given me any type of a feeling of home. I could never settle where each day was a struggle to just survive. I lean my head on Duke's shoulder. "Thank you for bringing me, but I'm ready to go back home."

I feel his lips press to the top of my head. "I'm glad we're on our way as well. Especially because we have a lengthy plane ride home."

I sit up and my stomach flips at what I see teasing in his eyes. "It is long," I agree and bite my lip to keep from laughing at the way his eyes flash with hidden meaning.

Duke helps me buckle into the leather seats of the Ainsworth jet. Never in a million years would I have dreamed I would be riding in anything this grand. I look up as the same flight attendant we had on the way over comes through the door at the front of the jet. Marissa is dressed in a navy skirt and blazer uniform, the Ainsworth crest embroidered on the front. Her blond hair is pulled back and pinned neatly.

"May I get you something to drink, Your Grace?" she asks.

"No, thank you, Marissa. Once we're in the air, we won't require any assistance unless I call for you."

"Certainly, sir." She nods and turns to leave.

As the door to the front of the jet clicks closed, Duke turns to me, his eyes dark and sensual, and my stomach clenches. "Once we're in the air, you're mine."

I swallow and shiver as a shot of adrenaline courses from my breasts straight to an ache between my legs. Our eyes connect and burn while the plane readies for takeoff. The engine roars to life, like the way my body is reacting under his heated gaze.

"Is this particular dress a favorite?" he asks, just as my stomach drops from the movement of the plane as it becomes airborne. I look down. "No. Not a favorite."

"Good." My gaze goes to the hard ridge outlined

through his slacks. "What have you done to me, Harlow? I can't ever seem to get enough."

I want him just as badly. There's a ding from the speakers above just before the captain comes on. "We've reached altitude, Your Grace. You may move freely about the cabin. We should reach Asheville in twelve hours and ten minutes."

Duke doesn't wait for the captain to finish before he unsnaps his seatbelt and then mine. Pulling me to my feet, his lips find mine, willing and anxious to meet his. He sweeps me into his arms and carries me to the couch, where he gently drops my feet into the plush carpet and runs his hands from my hips, over my breasts, and to the high neckline and rips the despicable garment down the middle.

I gasp, and my eyes flash to his. "That was so hot," I say, leaning into another kiss.

His hands wrap around my wrists. "Not yet, love. I need to see all of you."

With one flick of his hand, my bra falls to our feet. My panties soon follow. My eyes go nervously to the door to the cockpit. Standing completely naked in front of Duke, with him fully dressed, feels so bad yet so extremely exciting. My breath stops when he drops to his knees and takes one nipple into his mouth, swirling his tongue around the hardened nub. I begin to writhe beneath his touch, which earns me an exquisite nip of his teeth to my oversensitive nub. A burst of sensations spread through me like an overflowing river.

"Duke," I pant in a voice unrecognizable to me. "I need you."

His breath blows against my stomach as he moves his divine torture lower. My knees wobble. Without his hands holding me upright, I would collapse to the floor. Needing to touch him, I run my fingers through his dark, much-too-neatly-groomed hair. To my annoyance, he skips over the place where I want his kisses most and teases me by nipping the inside of my thighs with his lips, sending spiraling heat coursing to my very core. Higher and higher he torments me, until finally his breath warms my swollen folds. I dig my toes into the soft carpet when his tongue makes contact in a long, slow, wet lick along my crease.

My eyes flutter, and my head drops back as a slow, burning pleasure begins to build with each swipe of his tongue. My hands bury deeper in his hair to ground me to the earth. He pushes a finger inside just as my muscles began to contract. With a strong draw of his mouth on my clit, I come hard. My body shudders and shivers as each wave of pleasure ebbs through me. Never in my life have I felt so deeply connected to another.

Again, Duke sweeps me into his arms. I feel as if I'm floating, still held in post-orgasmic glow. He lays me gently on the bed, and his lips claim mine. I taste myself on his lips, and I need him again. My hands go to his shirt as I try to maneuver the buttons through the tiny holes, but it takes too much time. Just as he'd done to my dress, I grab the collar and rip it open, sending buttons flying. He bats my hands away from his belt and takes care of the task in only seconds, then he's covering my body with his. He reaches into a bedside table for protection, which he quickly rolls onto his length.

His hardened cock nudges my opening, and I spread my legs even wider, welcoming him in. This is what I need even more than my next breath. He takes my hands in his, entwining our fingers, and holds them over my head. Slowly he enters me, his gaze never leaving mine. I take pleasure from the desire smoldering in his eyes as he seats himself deeply inside of me. My emotions surge when he closes his eyes to simply enjoy our joining. It's the most incredible sight.

As he begins to thrust, I can no longer keep my focus on his handsome face. I wrap my legs around his waist and arch my body to bring him deeper inside me. My eyes flutter closed when it feels as if he touches my very womb. There is no warning, no tensing or muscle spasms to announce the arrival of my orgasm. I simply detonate, and a pleasure so intense shoots through me like a lightning strike in a summer rainstorm. I cry out, and Duke answers with moans of his own as he finds his own pleasure.

I tighten my legs around him, not wanting to miss a single pulse or contraction. He releases my hands to grab my hips, tilting me to a perfect angle to take his pulsing cock even deeper. Opening my eyes slowly as waves calm, I'm met by an unfamiliar emotion shining back at me from his eyes. An emotion that chills me to the bone:

love. Regret and sadness fill my heart. Even though he hasn't told me yet, I know our time together is limited. Adding love into our relationship is something I never anticipated, and it will only make our parting more painful in the end. I can feel myself start to pull back, listening to that tiny part of my heart that says, *"Run!"* But I know it's too late.

"I still can't believe you left before the royal wedding," Kaylee says.

Duke and I have been back home for a few days, but this is the first time we've all been able to get together. Kaylee flips the Tea Thyme sign to Closed. April and Rachael, along with Baylee, had come over to hear all about my trip and to restock my tea charm inventory. If their popularity continues, I'm going to have to make some changes. For the first time in forever, my bank account gives me a sense of security. Duke and I both know I could easily move out now, but neither one of us has mentioned it. Rachael even brought dinner and several bottles of wine. "Believe me, I didn't miss it. The one party I attended was plenty."

April tops off everyone's glass and says, "I still can't believe Duke is a duke."

"Me either. And he's related to royalty," Baylee says.

I swallow my sip of wine before saying, "Yeah, he is."

Rachael's eyes light with ire. "I'd like to spend ten

minutes with Duke's mother. She shouldn't be allowed to get away with treating you like that."

I'd told my friends about the warm reception I'd received from Mrs. Ainsworth. I just hadn't told them everything. What I overheard that day doesn't need to be re-told. Ever. "It's fine. She didn't tell me anything I didn't already know." I've begun to cherish every moment I have left with Duke. While he hasn't mentioned his impending move back to England, I can see he's been working through something.

April's eyes narrow. "Harlow, I see the way Duke looks at you. That man is smitten."

I laugh, and Rachael steps in to agree. "April's right. And he did ask you to move in."

I sigh and look around at my friends. Keeping my truths secret no longer matters to me. "About that…" I don't want to lie to them anymore. "I need to tell you all something. Something that I've been hiding from you."

Being the little mother that she is, Rachael takes my hands and says, "Oh, sweetie, what is it? You know you can tell us anything."

I nod and smile. I know what I have to tell them will paint me in a very bad light. But it's the light of truth, and there's no way around that. It's my life. "Kaylee, when I applied for a job, it was because I was homeless and only had a little money to my name."

Kaylee looks at me, frowning. "Harlow, why didn't you tell us? You could have stayed with any one of us."

Four sets of wounded eyes stare at me. "I didn't know you at the time, and then when I did get to know you, I was embarrassed to tell you."

"Where were you staying?" Rachael asks.

I struggle to admit the truth. "On the un-remodeled third floor of White Oaks. At first, I'd sneak in the door when someone went in. Then when Kaylee gave me a key card for deliveries, I used that. When I was sick, Duke found me and insisted I stay with him. That's why I'm living with Duke."

My friends look at each other, and I watch their reactions. All I see is love and understanding, and that makes my eyes wet.

"Can I ask how you found yourself homeless?" April asks.

I didn't want to lie anymore to my friends, but could I tell them about my dad? "I'm sorry. I'm just not ready to talk about that."

"You don't have to tell us anything; just know that we are all here for you. In fact, you can move into my guest house tonight if you'd like to," Rachael offers.

The thought makes me want to weep. "Maybe later. For now, I'm fine at Duke's." I'm not ready to leave Duke. Soon I'll have no choice but to leave, but for now, I want to hold on to every moment we have left.

"Kyle is going to be in Vegas next month. It would really help us out if you could housesit for us. You'd have the use of our cars for work," Rachael says.

"Thank you, Rachael. I'll think about it." I blink when I

feel pressure behind my eyes. These women are so incredible.

"You can live with me, Harlow," Baylee offers. I know she only has a one-bedroom apartment, and I wouldn't put her out like that, but it touches me that she'd offer without hesitation.

I smile, "Thanks, Baylee. I'll keep that in mind." I think my dad actually did me a favor by abandoning me near this town.

"So how did things go with you and Duke while you were in England?" Kaylee asks, as if the topic of my homelessness never happened.

"Yeah, could you see yourself as his Duchess?" April asks.

I shake my head. "No, never. First off, Mrs. Ainsworth would never allow that to happen. Plus, I don't think I would be happy living there. It seemed a very cold place." Except for the day I spent with Duke. He still hasn't mentioned his impending return. Yet, every night he makes sure I fall asleep exhausted. And every morning he takes me as I awaken, or he carries me into his shower, where he spends quality time making sure I'm clean. Everywhere. But I still feel like he's preoccupied with something.

"You look like you're trying to convince yourself of that," Kaylee says, and the others nod in agreement.

I shrug, "It's the way it has to be." They don't know that Duke's days in America are numbered. Soon he'll move back to England, marry, and produce the heirs that he must have. And it won't be with me. I wonder if it would be best if I did accept Rachael's offer to stay in her guesthouse. The longer I stay with Duke, the deeper I fall for him. Wouldn't it be smarter to back off now? Just the thought makes my heart race. *No.* Even though it would be smarter, I can't. Much too soon, he'll be lost to me.

The store phone rings, and Baylee runs to answer. She sticks her head out and says, "Harlow, you have a phone call."

My eyebrows pull together. *Who would be calling me?* "Thanks, Baylee," I say, taking the phone from her hand. I wait until she returns to the table before putting the phone to my ear. "Hello?"

"Harley, It's your dad."

As soon as I hear my dad's voice, I take the cordless phone and step out the back door into the alley behind the store. I know too well what this call will be like. They're always the same. I do sometimes wonder if I'm doing my dad a disservice by bailing him out each time he gets himself into trouble, but when I think of cutting him off, I remember that my mom would want me to look after him. "Dad. It's nice of you to call." I can't keep the bitterness from my voice.

"Don't be that way, baby girl," he says with a laugh.

I take a deep breath and try to remove the sting from my voice. "Are you all right, Dad?

"Sure. Sure, I'm fine," he answers, and I hope it's the truth.

"How did you find me?" I ask.

"I called the hotel where we stayed, and the lady that works there remembers you coming in to pay the bill. She said you gave her a necklace, and she knew where you worked because she bought another one from you. I'm happy to hear you're getting on so well." I hear so much more in his well-wishes.

"Yes, Barbara is a very nice lady." She's been a returning customer and has even sent several of her friends my way. But I know how my dad works, so I wait him out because I know it's coming. You'd think that, after abandoning your daughter and taking all of her possessions, you'd at least apologize, but I know that's a fruitless thought. At the very minimum, he could at least ask if I was okay. I know Dad loves me, but he's a self-centered person. I rub my eyes and sigh. I try to love him despite it.

"Honey, I need a little bit of help." I hear the desperation in his voice.

My heart sinks even lower. "What happened to my money in the trailer, Dad?" I ask, but I know it's gone.

"Well, about that... I had a real sure shot with a horse. I'd planned on doubling your money and surprising you with it."

It's always for me. "That's wonderful, Dad. When will I be getting it?"

He pauses, then his charm comes into play. "That's the thing. I stopped off to play the tables before the races and won big!"

I've heard this before. I'm waiting for it.

"Then I switched to blackjack, but the cards just weren't in my favor, and I lost it all."

I drop my head back against the brick wall. What can I do? He's my dad. "Okay, Dad. Just come back to North Carolina, and we'll figure something out."

"That's just it, baby girl. I already placed the bet on the ponies, and my horse came in sixth. Now I owe the bookie."

I close my eyes. The last time I heard that, we had to sell our home. "How much, Dad?"

"Twenty thousand dollars," he says.

"Dad!" I bark into the phone. I don't even have that much from everything I've made in my job and with my jewelry. The thought of starting over with nothing makes me nauseated.

"I know, I know. I'm sorry, baby." He sounds so remorseful, but I know it's all a ploy. "You just help me out this time, and I'll stop gambling altogether. I'll come get you, and we'll go on to Tennessee like we'd planned."

And now the bargaining promises start. "Dad, I can't send you that much money. I don't have it," I tell him. I only have about half that much, but I refuse to leave myself with nothing again.

"How much do you have?" he's quick to ask.

I sigh and look heavenward before answering. "I can send you about six."

"That's fine. I can sell the car for the rest of it. I promise you, this is the last time." I hear the certainty in his voice, as he believes what he's saying.

I'd worked so hard to buy that car. "I know, Dad. Tell me where to send it."

I know in my heart this isn't helping my dad at all. But I'm helpless to do anything but send him what I can. I end the call and slump back against the wall, slowly lowering until I'm sitting on the asphalt. I rest my head on my bent knees and let the tears come. I'm not crying over the lost money—I'm crying over the pain I know my father is in.

"Hey, there you are. Kaylee said you were out here," Duke says as he comes out the back door.

I quickly turn my head and wipe my eyes on the bottom on my uniform shirt.

"Harlow." Duke squats down and tips my head upward. "What's going on? Why are you crying?"

I sigh. This is so hard. "It's nothing." I don't want to admit the truth to Duke.

"Love, these tears aren't nothing." He swipes a tear from my cheek with his thumb.

Instead of answering him, I push to my feet and dust my bottom off. "It's nothing, really. Was there some reason you stopped by?"

He looks like he wants to push for an answer, and I'm thankful when he doesn't. "Fine. We'll ignore it for now, but I'm going to get answers. I stopped by to tell you I have to fly to New York and won't be back until tomorrow night."

I give him a weak smile. I'll miss him while he's gone. "Okay, thanks for letting me know."

He pulls me into his arms and give me a kiss that I didn't even know I needed so badly. I grasp his biceps through his suit and hang on as if I'm dangling from a perilous cliff and he's my savior. When he breaks the kiss, I give an anguished cry of painful loss. Duke presses my body closely to his, and I relax into the safety he gives me.

He takes my face in his hands and looks me in the eyes. "Love, tell me what's wrong. Let me help you."

Tears fill my eyes once again, and I nod slowly because I know I must tell him about my dad. "I will. Can we talk when you get back?"

He pulls me in for a hug. "I don't want to leave you like this."

I tip my head back and look up at him through watery eyes. "I'll be fine. Really, I will. I promise; we'll talk when you get home."

After one last kiss and a promise to call tonight, Duke reluctantly leaves. Before I can dry my eyes and get back to work, Baylee steps out the back door.

"Hey, Harlow," Baylee says with a huge smile on her face.

Just seeing her makes me smile. I love Baylee. "Hi, Baylee. I was just coming back in."

She nods. "I know. I saw Duke leave. But you're upset. Is his business trip making you sad? You can come over to my apartment for the night. We'll have popcorn and watch movies," she says, her eyes bright and hopeful.

Baylee is the most sensitive and sweetest person I've ever known. She can pick up on emotions quickly. It's almost like she feels them herself. Kaylee finally told me that Baylee has some cognitive and learning disabilities. I've never seen any evidence of this in the months I've been working here, other than her deep compassion for others. "No, honey. He didn't make me sad. I got a call from my dad that made me sad."

Baylee frowns. "Fathers shouldn't make their children sad."

I give her shoulders a squeeze. "No, sweetie, they shouldn't, but sometimes they can't help it."

She looks right into my eyes as she says, "That's when you have to love your dad the most and do the thing that's right. Even if it hurts." If I didn't know better, I'd think Baylee was clairvoyant.

The right thing to do would be to tell my dad that he's on his own in solving his gambling problems. But if I do that, it could lead to him being physically hurt. It's happened in the past. And what if I withhold money from my dad, and he's killed because of his debts? It could happen. And if that were to happen, I'd never be able to forgive myself. "You're right, Baylee. But that isn't always easy to do."

"Do you want to come with me this afternoon when I

walk Mr. Boots? Doggie kisses always make me feel better."

I smile at her simple answer. Baylee started walking a few dogs in the apartment complex when she found out that they have to stay by themselves during the day. She said they get lonely. It's turning into a lucrative business, and along with keeping her neighbor's daughter after school and helping out at Tea Thyme, it helps her keep the independence to live on her own. I understand from Kaylee that Baylee fought long and hard to get her parents to agree to her moving out of their family home.

"That sounds like fun, but I think I'll pass for now."

She grins and nods. "Okay."

Before we go in, I stop Baylee. "Thanks, Baylee."

She gives me an encouraging hug. "I love you, Harlow. If you need a place to stay, you can always stay with me."

Since I don't go in to work until the afternoon, I pop over to Tea Thyme and ask Kaylee to borrow her car. I drive into Treemont and wire my hard-earned cash to the number dad gave me. Once that's done, I return Kaylee's car to the alley behind the shop. I go back to Duke's home and try to keep my mind off the fact that he's not just down in his office but rather out of the state.

I have a lot of decisions to make. The first and foremost is living with Duke. Mr. Compton said Duke's return would occur soon, but I have no idea how soon that may be. I can't depend on living here much longer. Now, after sending my dad money, I no longer have the means to get my own apartment. I could stay in Rachael's guest house, but that's a last resort.

And then there's my jewelry business. I go upstairs to the studio Duke set up for me and log into the computer he's been letting me use. I check my website and find more orders. I wonder if I'm at the point where I could stop working at Tea Thyme and go full-time into my designs. I'm not sure what I should do. But with Kaylee, I have the security of knowing I have a paycheck. So maybe I should wait.

Before I log out, I notice my inbox has several new messages. I re-read the emails several times before I believe them. Then I wonder if they are real. One is from a bride in Asheville who wants to commission me to make a dozen necklace and earring sets for her wedding party. Her budget is three thousand dollars! She wants to meet with me and pick out a design and colors. I reply that I'd be happy to meet with her. I'm sure Kaylee will let me borrow her car.

The second email is from the CEO of the most popular coffee and tea store in America. They would like to discuss my tea charms. I don't even stop to think as I pick up the phone and push the programed button to call Duke. The phone rings and eventually sends me to his voicemail. Duke always answers my calls. He's just busy. That's why he went to New York. But in the back of my mind, a crazy thought takes root: His mother said he'd lose interest... *No. I'm not letting that woman's hurtful words ruin what time I have left with Duke. He's just busy. I'll tell him when he gets home tomorrow.*

I power off the laptop and run my hand over the boxes of colorful beads. I flip open several, and a wedding design is already forming in my mind. It comforts me to pick up the same tools that were once in my mom's hands. It's almost like she's with me, giving me strength. Many hours later, I'm extremely weary, but I'm proud of the necklace and earring set I created.

It's well after three in the morning before I lay my head down on the pillow in Duke's bed. I've never slept in his bed alone. I had even considered sleeping in one of his guest rooms, but I wanted to feel him around me. He hadn't called like he said he would. My imagination wasn't helping. His scent still remains on the sheets. I hold his pillow to my face and inhale then burst into tears. I feel the end coming.

CHAPTER FIFTEEN

Duke

I switch the bouquet of flowers in my arms and rub the back of my neck as I ride up to my penthouse in the elevator. I was late getting back, and I hope Harlow isn't already in bed. I'd intended to call her the night before, but meetings ran late, and then the investor moved us all to his yacht, where I didn't have cell reception. I hadn't gotten back to the room until after midnight, and I knew it was too late to call.

I find her standing by the windows, looking out over the lights of the town. My cock hardens when I see her wrapped in one of my dress shirts, like a caress to her body. She turns, and just like always, our eyes connect on a deeper level. She holds out her arms to me, and I drop the flowers on the floor and replace them with her warm body.

"I'm sorry—" I try to say, but she stops me with a finger to my lips.

"Make love to me, Duke," she says with a desperation I've never heard.

I kiss her, taking my time to explore and consume every inch of her lips and mouth. I groan when I open my shirt and find that she's wearing absolutely nothing underneath. "You're so beautiful, love."

I push the garment from her shoulders and drop to my knees before her. Grasping one delectable cheek in each hand I bring her to my face and breathe her in. I'm finally home. With my tongue, I drink in her juices and lap at the swollen nub I find hidden within her folds. Her hands run through my hair, and she pulls my head closer to her. The frantic sounds she's making almost send me over the edge.

I should take my time. I should draw this out and give her everything I have, but I can't. I need her too badly. I missed her greatly. Adding one and then two fingers inside of her, I search for the spot that I know will take her over. I feel her muscles quiver, and with a final hard draw on her clit, she comes around my fingers. I twirl her around and press her against the windows looking out to the town below us. I know that no one can see us. There are no other buildings in the distance, but I can tell by the juice running down her leg that just the thought of being caught makes her hot.

"Keep your hands on the glass, spread your legs, and bend over for me, love. I need to be inside you." Quickly, I roll on a condom. Her breasts are pressed against the window, and with one smooth, hard thrust, I enter her with a groan. "You feel so incredible." I want to stay lost in her depths forever.

"Don't stop," she pleads.

I pull out and thrust back in. "No. Never. Not until you scream my name."

With each thrust, I grasp her tighter and tighter, my fingers gripping her hips. I want to own her. Claim her as mine. She's perfect. She screams my name at the exact moment I realize she's mine.

Later, after I carried her to our bed and gave her more than a handful of orgasms, I lay awake with my mind unable to shut down. Duty and desire are warring in my head. Duty to a position I never asked for or wanted but was born into. And my desire of having Harlow in my life.

She hated England. My mother doesn't approve of her. Mum would make Harlow's life a living hell. I can't do that to her. She deserves happiness, and I don't think she would ever be happy as my Duchess. She's even said as much.

I turn on my side to watch her sleep. Her dark-blonde hair feathers over her face. I gently brush it back, and she stirs, seeking my body even in her sleep. I wrap my arms around her and pull her into my chest, kissing the top of her head. She snuggles in, never waking.

I haven't told her of the deal I'd made with my mum or

that my time in America, at least on the scale it's been, will be over before Christmas. Like an impending doom, I know the best thing for Harlow is to let her go. Above all, I want her happiness. I want her safe, and I want her to have a happy life. As much as I selfishly want that to be with me, I don't think it's possible.

First thing tomorrow, I need to find out what that phone call from her father was about. Something upset her, and I'm going to get to the bottom of it. Then, as much as it cuts my heart, I need to leave and return to England early. Staying will only make our parting that much harder.

Just before sleep claims me, I feel Harlow's lips on mine, her nipples hard and abrasive against my chest. As naturally as I take my next breath, I roll over and sink into her. She quickly comes, and as I thrust the final time and spend myself within her walls, I feel as if I've lost the most important thing in my life. I've lost my happiness.

The next morning, I'm dressed and waiting for Harlow at the breakfast table. She's a ray of sunshine as she walks into the room in a yellow-and-orange print wraparound dress. I hate what I'm about to do. She wraps her arms around me, but I keep my arms by my side and don't return the hug, nor do I kiss her upturned lips. Her eyes narrow in question.

"I was hoping you'd still be in bed when I woke," she smiles and says.

"I had business to attend to this morning." Her head tips, questioning my brisk answer.

It takes everything I have inside of me to walk away from her. "I must hurry. After you finish, would you please come to my office?"

Her eyes grow uneasy. "Of course. Is something wrong?" she asks, her voice filled with concern.

"Later," I answer shortly. "Eat breakfast, then we'll talk." I'm almost at the door when she calls out.

"Duke." I turn back around, and she asks, "Have I done something wrong?"

My mistake was in turning around. I see the hurt in her eyes from my cold treatment. I should still be lying beside her in bed after what we shared last night, but I have to do this...for her. "No. I'll see you later."

It was obvious by the fallen look on her face that I'd already begun to hurt her.

"Please take a seat," I say when Harlow walks in my office thirty minutes later. Tension pulls at the edges of her eyes, and her arms are wrapped around her body as if she's cold, but I know it's to close me out. On some level she knows.

"Duke, you're scaring me. Why are you acting like this?" she asks, pleading with her eyes for me to break the coldness I'm surrounding myself with.

"First, I need to know about your phone call. Who was on the phone that upset you?"

Her eyes widen. "That's what you're upset about?"

Her eyes bore into mine. "How can I be upset when I have no idea what your call was about or who it was from?"

She sits back in the chair, and her head drops. "The call was from my father." She sighs heavily and looks toward the window, I'm sure wishing she were out there instead of in here being drilled for answers. My anger at her father has grown in proportions as her story unfolds.

"As long as I can remember, my father has had a problem with gambling. When my mom was alive, he kept everything mostly under control. But when we lost her, he tried, really tried, to beat it, but it was too easy for him to escape the pain of losing her in gambling. We lost our house and the college money they had saved since I was born to pay off his debt. He tried to work, but it was hard for him to keep a job. Over the years, he'd have periods of good times when he could fight the temptation, but then he'd fall. For the last two years, he'd been really good. I thought moving away from Atlantic City would help him. We packed up a trailer and headed to Tennessee. I had an aunt that lived there once, and we really liked the area.

"When we got to Treemont, we stopped for the night at a hotel off of Highway 40. I went to go get us something to eat, and when I came back, he was gone. He'd taken every-thing with him. That's why you found me living on the third floor. I didn't have any other options. I'd saved for ten years and had over ten thousand dollars, but he took that as well. I had nothing. Not even my cellphone."

I knew it would be bad, but I never anticipated this. "And the call the other day was from your father?"

She bites her lip and nods. "Yes. He was in trouble with a bookie and wanted me to send him money."

I take a breath to lessen the rage I feel toward her father. "How much?" I ask.

Her complexion has gone ever paler. "Six thousand. But I don't want you to think this is your problem. It's not. It's my problem, and I've handled it."

I don't even respond to that. There's nothing she can do. The woman before me is so much stronger that I ever imagined. "Do you know where your father is now?" I can't leave her with this over her head. I have to fix at least this much of her life before I go.

She looks down at her hands and slowly shakes her head. "No. I just have the number that I wired the money to."

"I will need that number," I tell her.

"Why?" Her eyes search mine and then begin to fill with tears.

"Because it appears my time in America has come to an end sooner than I'd anticipated. I don't want to leave you with problems over your head. I'll take care of your father. You'll stay in the penthouse, and I've set you up with a bank account that should hold you over until you are on your feet again. I'm also leaving Jeffrey and the staff in place. Ms.

Bennett has a household budget, so just tell her when you need something."

Her face turns ashen, and I see the hurt in her eyes, hurt that I'm causing. "What? Wait. I don't want any of that. I just want you."

My heart is breaking right along with hers. "Harlow, think very hard about this. If you are with me, you know what that will include. Can you honestly see yourself as my duchess?" I wait silently for her answer. If she says yes, then I'll move heaven and earth to make that happen.

Her eyes leave mine, and she looks down, wiping her tears away with a finger. I feel her leaving me. Shutting me out. "Last night was our last time together, wasn't it?" she asks quietly.

I press my lips together before answering. "Yes."

She doesn't say anything, but I can see she's working through something in her mind. "You knew about this last night, so it was a goodbye fuck, then."

My body jerks as if she'd hit me. I want to demand she take it back, those horribly untrue words. What we shared last night was anything but a goodbye fuck. "Yes. I need an heir, as my mum has pointed out on numerous occasions, so I'm leaving today to pursue that."

I see her back straighten, just like she's had to do on so many occasions in her life. Her strength will get her through. I have to believe that. I push a folder of papers toward her. "This is your banking account and cards. Please let Ms. Bennett know if you need anything else. She knows how to contact my London office."

With that, I pick up my satchel and walk out. I hear a strangled cry behind me, but I don't stop, and I don't turn back. When the elevator doors close on me for the last time, tears are marring my own cheeks.

CHAPTER SIXTEEN

Harlow

I sit in Duke's office long after he's gone. Whether I'm in shock or simply numb from the onslaught I've just had, I'm not sure, nor does it matter. The outcome is the same. Duke is gone. I press my hands to my mouth to keep from crying out. I notice he left everything in his office, as if he'd be coming back. But... My eyes dart to the shelf where he stored the silly little gifts I'd left him. They were just little things I'd found in the dumpsters or on trips to the second-hand store. I'd probably spent less than five bucks on everything, and he'd taken them all. My hand swipes over the empty shelf. More tears fall from my eyes. He took them with him. I turn my head and look in the window where the sun-catcher I'd made once hung. It's gone as well. My knees will no longer hold me, and I sink to the floor.

Somehow, I make my way back to the penthouse and get ready for work. I can't afford to let my emotions take control of me. I'll fall apart later, but for now I've got to hold it together. As I step from the closet, pulling my uniform top over my head, my eyes drift to our bed. Duke's bed. It was never mine. I realize I can't stay here. Not even another night. I search the bathroom cabinets for trash bags and stuff only the clothes I'd purchased inside. It only takes two pitiful bags to hold my possessions. On my way out, I gaze up the stairs that lead to the studio. I'll have to leave my beads until I know where I'm going.

As soon as I walk into Tea Thyme, Kaylee takes one look at me and motions for me to follow her through to the kitchen.

She wraps her arms around me and asks, "Who died?"

I let my tears fall and hold on to her like a life raft in a raging sea. She doesn't try to stop me; she lets me cry it out while making comforting sounds that eventually slow my tears and calm my broken heart. I sniff back the remaining tears. "I can't talk about it now. But can you call the girls to meet us after work? I need to talk to everyone."

"We're not waiting. This is an emergency." Within an hour, Kaylee has the Closed sign on Tea Thyme, and she, April, Rachael, and Baylee sit staring at me with such concern in their eyes that it floors me. I've only known these four women a short time, yet they feel as close to me as sisters.

"Thank you all for coming so quickly," I say, and Baylee stands up and gives me another hug. I smile even though I'm in pain.

"Honey, you know we'd do anything for you. You're one of us now," April says, reaching over to give my hand a squeeze.

I can't help the tear that runs down my cheek. "Thank you. When I came to Treemont, I never expected to find such wonderful friends. I've been keeping a lot from you, and I'm really sorry."

Then I tell them everything. This time I leave nothing out. By the time I'm finished, I'm completely drained.

"Duke just left you?" Rachael asks, fire lighting her eyes.

I can't believe how awesome my friends are. They completely skipped over the part about my dad's gambling. "Yeah. He's gone back to England."

"To marry a duchess and have an heir?" Baylee asks.

I grin. "Yeah, Bay."

April throws up her hands and says, "He's an asshole!"

Everybody agrees, and I love these women even more.

"So, what are you going to do now?" Rachael asks.

I smile and ask, "If it's not too much of an imposition, could I stay in your guest house? I'll pay you as much rent as I can."

Rachael's is quick to answer. "Yes, the guesthouse is

yours for as long as you want it, but I won't hear of you paying rent. That's what friends are for. And we have more than enough vehicles in our garage, so you can take your pick."

I sniffle again. Not from Duke leaving, but because I have such a strong support team surrounding me. "That's very generous. Can I move in tonight? I can't stay in the penthouse one second longer."

"Of course you can. Is that what's in the garbage bags?" Rachael asks.

I bow my head and nod. "Thank you."

"Come on, let's get you settled. We'll open a bottle of wine and think of ways to torture and maim Duke or Oliver or whatever his name is."

That gets a smile out of me.

The next morning, I hear a knock on the door of Rachael's guest house. I open it only to find Jeffrey with all my jewelry tools and supplies. "Jeffrey, how did you know where to find me?" I ask.

"Good morning, Ms. Davidson. Ms. Bennett called to say you didn't return to the penthouse last night. We were all concerned. Ms. Conrad at Tea Thyme told me you had moved here. We all thought you'd need your things. I do have the rest of your clothes, your computer, and other things you left."

I feel so bad. He does look like he'd been concerned. "I'm sorry I worried you all. You can bring my jewelry supplies in, but I don't want the other things. You can return them or you can donate them, but as far as I'm concerned, they don't belong to me."

He nods, "Where would you like me to put your tools?" he asks, and I hear disapproval in his voice. At least as much as he could disapprove and still maintain his professional demeanor. I don't know what Duke told his employees, but I suppose it's normal for them to take his side.

I show him in and direct him to the second bedroom. It has the best light, and I can pull a table in to work on. I want to ask him if he's heard from Duke, but I don't. Maybe I don't want to know how he is. When he leaves, I can't stop a new batch of tears. That was my last connection to Duke.

The next week, I use one of Rachael's cars and drive into Asheville to meet Julie Montgomery and discuss her designs for her wedding. Two hours later, I leave her house with a fifteen-hundred-dollar check in my bag, and an order for twelve matching sets of necklaces and earrings.

I work for the next two weeks to complete them, and when I deliver them, she pays me the other fifteen hundred. It was hard to accomplish while working full time at Tea Thyme, but I'm still not ready to give up the security of that paycheck.

Each day that goes by, I miss Duke. Each night that I lie in bed without him, I cry. But I know this is best. As each day goes by, I try to survive and find my way without him.

I've stressed and worried so much I've begun to have bouts of nausea hit me out of the blue.

I'm at work the next week, when I get another phone call from my dad.

"Hello, Dad." I wait to hear what mess I have to clean up now.

"Baby. I called to tell you how much I love you."

This does not sound like my dad. His voice is stronger, clearer, and without the defeated sound I'm used to hearing. And he said he loved me. He hasn't said those words since before Mom died. My skin grows cold. Is he sick? Or dying? "Dad, are you all right?"

"I'm fine, Harley girl. I'm better than I've been in a lot of years, and I have that young man of yours to thank for it," he says.

My what? "Who?" I ask.

"Oliver came to see me," my dad says.

My heart starts to race at just hearing his name. "He did? When?"

"About a month ago. He opened my eyes to a lot of my mistakes in life. One being how I've treated you since your mom died. I'm sorry, baby. I'm sorry I wasn't there for you." His voice cracks, thick with emotion.

"Dad, what's going on?" I have to sit down on a work stool before my knees give out.

"Oliver set me up in a rehab center. I've been working through my problems."

Tears fill my eyes. Why would Duke do that? Why

would he help my dad? "That's wonderful, Dad. I'm very proud of you."

"I owe you so much, Harlow. I'm ashamed of how I've acted since your mom left us."

"Oh, no, Dad. You don't owe me anything." Tears gather in my eyes.

"Yes, I do. Don't cut me any slack. I've been shit as a father, but I'm working on it. I'm not there yet, but someday I hope you'll forgive me and let me back into your life."

I smile and close my eyes, causing the tears filling them to run down my cheeks. "I'd like that, Dad. I'd like that so much."

Kaylee found me later in the kitchen, crying my eyes out. But this time with a smile.

The next day, I'm working in the back when Baylee sticks her head in the door and says, "Harlow, you have a visitor."

I look up, my brows pinched together. "I do? Who is it?"

She shrugs, "I have no idea, but he looks official."

Official? I wonder what that means. It doesn't take me long to discover exactly what she meant. The gentleman waiting for me looks like he'd just stepped out of Wall Street. He was maybe in his fifties, with more pepper than salt in his neatly trimmed and styled hair. He reminds me a bit of Duke.

I cautiously walk up to him and say, "Hello, I'm Harlow Davidson. How may I help you?"

"Good afternoon, Ms. Davidson. I'm Martin Bradford,"

he says with a smile as he shakes my hand then holds out a business card. I glance down and see the logo for the coffee shop that had emailed me about my tea charms.

"You're from Green Bean?" I ask.

He nods. "Yes. I wonder if you would have a few moments to talk."

I look up and see Kaylee only a few feet away, ready to jump in if I need her. I smile, and she nods with a wink, which makes me smile back.

"Sure," I say, and point to a table near the back. "Is this okay?" I ask.

"That will be fine." He waits for me to lead the way.

"Can I get you anything to drink or eat? We have some really good bear claws today."

He chuckles at the name. "No, nothing for me, but thank you." He waits until I sit before he takes the seat across from me. He pulls a few papers out of a folder I hadn't noticed him holding.

"What is this about, Mr. Bradford?" I ask.

"As we stated in our email, we're very serious about purchasing your tea charm concept. We have a preliminary offer for you." He pushes a paper to my side of the table.

My eyes scan the document. I don't really understand some of the legal terms, but the amount given causes me to choke on my saliva. I start coughing and gasp for breath. My eyes fix on the number of zeros written after the number two.

Kaylee runs and hands me a cup of water. My eyes

water and I work for each short panting breath. "Is this a joke?" I croak.

The corners of his eyes crinkled. "I can assure you it isn't. We wouldn't offer that amount unless we believed in the success of the product. Now, as I've said, this is only a preliminary offer. I would like to propose you and your counsel meet with us at our New York office to hammer out all the particulars. We, of course, will cover all travel expenses."

"Mr. Bradford, you have completely shocked me. I'm going to need time to think about this."

Kaylee steps and quickly says, "No, she doesn't. When do you want her there?"

Mr. Bradford's eyes go from Kaylee back to me, waiting for me to respond. I finally nod. "How about by the end of the week? I'll get my assistant to make the reservations," he says before I can change my mind.

"Excellent," Kaylee answers for me. She shakes Mr. Bradford's hand as he leaves, and I'm still staring at the numbers on the paper.

As soon as the door closes, Kaylee pulls me up, and we both jump up and down screaming as every customer in the store claps. My first coherent thought is to call Duke and share the news with him, but then I remember, and tears fill my eyes. Just that quickly, my euphoria turns into sadness.

"Ah, honey. Come here." Kaylee pulls me in for a hug. She knows what the tears are for. "It will get better."

Sniffling, I shake my head, smearing my tears on her

uniform top. "I don't know, Kay. It hurts as much today as it did the day he left."

~

Friday morning, I'm boarding the plane, in a new three-piece women's business suit. The fuchsia pencil skirt and jacket were tailored to fit me perfectly. April and Rachael had taken me into Asheville to purchase power suits for my trip. Gosh, those girls. What would I do without them? I'd spent almost everything I'd made from the wedding pieces, but if this deal really does go through, I'll never have to worry about money again.

It's ironic. I'd give up every bit of the money I'm going to make on this deal if I could have Duke. I'm starting to see our relationship in a whole new light. Duke rescued me when I needed him the most. But I think he needed me just as much. I feel as if I've grown in the month since we parted. I'm much more confident in myself and in my abilities to survive and to prosper. Duke had a lot to do with that transformation. He believed in me from the start, and now I've finally caught on. I believe in me, too.

The flight was quick and uneventful. Nothing like my luxurious flight to England on Duke's private plane. I leave the plane, pulling my new carry-on behind me. Just like in the movies, I see a gentleman in a suit holding a sign in front of him with my name on it. That must be Mr. Porter.

Kyle put me in touch with his lawyer, who I guess is now my lawyer, too.

"Hi, I'm Harlow Davidson," I say as I step in front of him.

"It's nice to meet you, Ms. Davidson. I'm Michael Porter." He offers his hand, and we shake. "Let me get that for you, and we'll be on our way to our meeting."

He reaches for my suitcase, but I say, "It's okay. I've got it. Just lead the way."

We arrive at the lawyer's office and are shown into a glass-walled conference room. An hour later, we leave, and I'm walking on air.

On the ride down in the elevator, Mr. Porter says, "You are one fierce negotiator, Ms. Davidson."

My eyes tear when I hear that word. Nobody but Duke has ever called me fierce. I sniffle and smile. "Thank you."

I negotiated for a base payment and a percentage of the profit, instead of selling them the trademarked concept like they'd first offered. I'll still be involved with the design of the charms, just not the production or marketing.

"Officially, my duties as your lawyer are over, so I wondered if you'd like to go out to dinner with me tonight," Mr. Porter asks with a practiced smile.

My eyes draw together. He's asking me out? "Like on a date?" I ask just to be sure we're on the same page.

His eyes warm, and he smiles. "Yes. A date. I find you a very interesting woman, Harlow Davidson. I'd like to get to know the woman behind the unique name."

This is the first time in years that a man has found me attractive and has asked me out on a date. He's quite handsome in his business suit. He's tall but not as tall as…some. His hair is a light brown, almost blond in places, and he wears it in a very neat style with a side part, the top longer and smoothed back. His eyes are brown, not blue, and his chin is almost oval, not strong and angular. And I'm in no way attracted to him. Not even a little.

I smile to soften the blow. I'm sure he's probably not used to being turned down. "Thank you for the invitation, but I believe I'll just go to the hotel and order room service. I've never done that before."

He nods slowly and pauses before asking, "Is there someone else?"

I sigh, "No. Not now. But there was. I'm sorry, I'm just not ready."

Our gazes meet, and I can see in his eyes that he understands. I wonder who hurt him. He surprises me by saying, "I understand. How about this—I know a great New York pizza place around the corner. How about going to celebrate your deal? As friends."

I smile and nod, "I'd like that."

A month later, I'm still living in Rachael's guesthouse. I could easily buy a home, but I like it here, and it helps Rachael and Kyle out when they have to travel.

I've had a lot of time to think about the way Duke left, and I've concluded that Duke didn't want to go, but he knew he had to. In my heart, I believe he wanted to stay with me. I choose to believe that he did have feelings for me. But he also had a duty to his family. His loyalty was one of the things that attracted me to him. He couldn't turn his back on his heritage. I remember the day he left. He asked me to think about being his duchess, and I had the odd feeling he wanted me to answer yes.

I scour the online news daily to see if a wedding announcement for the Duke of Ainsworth is featured. So far, I've found nothing more than a few pictures of Duke and his mother. I know it will cut deeply when I read about his upcoming nuptials. I only hope his mother lets him select his bride. And I hope his bride will make him happy.

I sit down at the kitchen table, where I've spread out my bead work, when I hear a knock at the door.

"Come in," I call out as Baylee blows in. Baylee's dog-walking business has grown into a doggie daycare, now that the young girl she babysat moved.

As I am getting used to, Baylee gives me a big hug, first thing. "I came to get your packages to mail."

"Right. Thanks, Baylee." I'd been having Baylee pick up my jewelry orders and take them to the post office. It helps her out and me as well. These days, it's all I can do to drag myself out of bed.

Baylee studies my face and then says, "You're sad, Harlow. Are you still sad because you can't be with Duke?"

LIZABETH SCOTT

Tears fill my eyes with no warning. I brush one away with my thumb and tell her the truth. "Yeah, Bay. I still miss him."

"You should go be with him, then you'd be happy." She says that like it's just so simple.

I grin. She's right. I would be happy then. "Duke lives in England, for one thing." I try to explain.

She stops to think, then says, "So you love Treemont more than Duke?"

"What? No, that's not it. He's a duke. That's like royalty, and if we were to marry, then that would make me a duchess." She just can't understand how impossible that would be.

Her eyes soften and go all dreamy. "That sounds like a fairytale to me."

I smile. "Yeah, it does," I admit.

She nods like she's finally figured it out. "And you don't want a fairytale life with the man you love?" she asks, her eyes fixed on my face, waiting for my answer.

"No. I don't…" I say and feel sick to my stomach. I let myself give into my fears and insecurities and consequentially lost the very best thing in my life. Duke had given me so much of himself, and when he needed me to step up and take my place beside him, I'd turned and run, using my feelings of inadequacy as an excuse.

Baylee puts her hand on my stomach, and I don't think anything about it. Baylee is touchy. "So why can't you be with him?" she smiles and asks.

Baylee has no idea that she's just caused a major break-through in my life. "I don't really know." How could I have been so blind? "What if it's too late?" I ask Baylee.

She shrugs her shoulders and grins. "What if it's not?" she counters.

She's right. I'll never know unless I try. Will he forgive me? I love Duke, and I want to marry him. I'll fight every day if I have to, in order to claim my place beside him. After all, I am fierce. My stomach flips. Am I really going to do this? Yes, I must. I press my hand to my stomach as it starts to heave, and I take a few deep breaths.

"Are you okay, Harlow? You look kinda green," she says, running her fingers through my hair and brushing it back from my face much like a mother would to a sick child.

I take a few deep breaths, and the swirling feeling does seem to calm. "I might be coming down with a tummy bug. I've not been feeling very well lately."

She takes my hand and leads me over to the couch. "Sit down on the couch and let me get you something to drink."

I lower myself to the couch, being careful to move slowly.

Baylee rushes back in with a sleeve of crackers and a drink. "Here, I found some saltine crackers and ginger ale. That's really good to settle a pregnant stomach," she says, holding both out to me.

I chuckle. "Oh, I'm not pregnant, Baylee," I say. Then an imaginary calendar runs through my mind. When was my last period? It was… It was… Another flash of memory. The last time we were together. The morning he left. I woke him up and he…and then we… We didn't use protection. My hand goes to my stomach. Could it be possible? Shouldn't I be freaking out? But I realize I'm not. I'm calm and in control, and I know what I want. I know *who* I want.

CHAPTER SEVENTEEN

Duke

"I really think you should consider Alysia Rushforth. She comes from an outstanding family. I had Rogert check into their background, and they're blemish-free other than a few minor transgressions. But who doesn't have a few of those in their closets? She would make a very good match for you. Then there is…"

I let my mother drone on about the available women she's vetted as my duchess. None of them interest me. My eyes catch the movement of the trees swaying in the wind from the window behind my mother's position on the couch. The view from my office is nothing like the mountain vista from my office at White Oaks. There, I had a panoramic view of several mountain ranges. I miss those mountains.

That's not all I miss, but I can't think of her without my heart breaking a little bit more. I know I did the right thing. Harlow would have been miserable here. Unconsciously, I reach for the tape dispenser sitting prominently on my desk. I worry how she's doing. Ms. Bennett said she moved out the day I left, and Ms. Sheldon said she hasn't touched any of the money or accounts I set up for her. She won't even let me take care of her to ease my guilty conscience.

"I wish you'd get rid of that garish thing, Oliver. It's embarrassing."

I gaze at the whimsical green frog in my hand. I hadn't even realized I'd picked it up. Its black bug eyes glare at me while it sticks its tongue out in a very accusing manner. Get rid of it? Never.

"It's that girl, isn't it?" I hear the bite of disapproval in Mum's voice.

I sigh and open a desk drawer to put Froggy in, as I no longer trust him in plain sight. I give a long-suffering sigh before saying, "She has a name, Mum." I'm so tired of my mum's negativity toward Harlow. Even now that she's won —*especially* now that she's won.

"I'm just glad you came to your senses. She would never have worked out for you." She shuffles through pages of hopefuls and moves a few to the top of the stack. Lucky them. None of them will suit me. But Harlow would. She would have been perfect for me. "Why, Mum? Why was Harlow such a bad choice?"

Her expression turns sour. "She has no breeding or manners. She would be unable to take her place beside you in society. You need a refined woman who knows how to get along with the upper class."

"And that's important?" I ask, curious for her answer, because what my mum describes sounds to me like an advert for a dog.

She looks up, visibly annoyed, and says, "Well, of course it is."

I love my mum. I always will, but I also know her faults. She's had a difficult life, even before Father died. The one thing that's always been steadfast is that she always has my best interests at heart. It's confusing to me why she doesn't now. "But my happiness means nothing as long as we appear to be the perfect family."

Again, our eyes meet. "Duty comes before happiness, Oliver."

That sounds like a well-practiced answer. "Did you love Father?" I ask, because I don't remember seeing evidence of that growing up. They always had their own things to do.

She clears her throat before answering, as if she trying to come up with an acceptable answer. "I came to have a fondness for him. I miss him dearly. I suppose we grew to love each other."

That sounds cold to me. "You didn't love him when you married?"

Her posture relaxes as she twists her wedding rings nervously. She still wears them, so doesn't that mean she felt something for him? I don't think I've ever seen Mum so unsure and human. "Our fathers came to the agreement that a marriage between us would be mutually beneficial."

"So, your marriage was based on a business decision and not on who you loved." Cold and impersonal. The same thing she wants for me.

Her face softens, and her eyes take on a misty, faraway look. "Sometimes love isn't enough," she says quietly. Her hands stop twisting her rings.

"But if you could have married for love, instead of what looked good on paper or in the news, or what your parents wanted you to do, would you have done so?" I ask, because I really want to know her answer. Fate had given us our position in society. Is there never a possibility for happiness?

She doesn't answer right away. In fact, I'm not sure she's going to answer at all. My mum's stern exterior looks to be cracking. "I did have a beau, long before your father, but I wasn't strong enough to go against my father's wishes."

I'm stunned. I take a good look at my mum. Not through the eyes of her son, but through the eyes of an adult. She's only just reached her fifty-first year, and she's still a very attractive woman. Has she ever had control over her own life? "Do you regret it? Marrying Father, I mean."

Without a thought, she shakes her head. "Never." Her

eyes water, but she smiles and says, "Because I have you, and that, I will never regret."

I go to her and kneel at her feet like I used to do as a child. I take her hands and look her directly in the eyes. "I love Harlow, Mum."

She sighs, removing her glasses, making her blue eyes appear even bluer. I can see her working through accepting what I said. She turns her eyes to mine, pats my cheek, and smiles with complete understanding. "Then, I suppose you should go get her. We'll make it work."

Then I remember the reason I left, and my momentary joy turns once again to sorrow. "She doesn't want this. She was miserable when we visited. I can't see her unhappy and in a position that doesn't give her happiness."

"I'm afraid I had a lot to do with making her stay unpleasant," Mum admits.

My brow rises. "What did you do, Mum?"

Mum stands, and I do as well. "Go and get your true love, son, and I will make this right. I owe Harlow an apology." She gathers her things and pauses before heading to the door. "And...I think it's time I move to the Dowager house," she announces.

For the first time since I left Harlow over two months ago, I feel a spark of happiness. I kiss my mum on the cheek as she leaves then return to my desk to formulate a plan. Before I can even log on to my computer, my office phone rings.

"Your Grace, you have a visitor," my assistant announces.

I don't remember a meeting scheduled for this morning, but I've not been my usual self lately. I probably forgot. "Send them in please, Mr. Bingham."

I blink when the door opens, because I'm obviously hallucinating. She stands just inside the doorway, looking nothing like the last time I saw her. This woman is dressed to perfection. Her curls have been tamed into a style that, combined with her black pencil skirt, green blouse, and jacket make her look like a fashionable businesswoman. My eyes go to her feet. She's even wearing stiletto heels. "Harlow?" I ask, just to verify.

She breezes in and offers her hand. I shake it because I'm too confused to form a rational thought. "Good afternoon, Your Grace. I wonder if I may have a bit of your time? I do apologize for not scheduling an appointment, but I was afraid you wouldn't see me."

What has she done with my Harlow? My lips crack into a grin. I'll play her game. "Of course, please come in." I want to go to her and take her in my arms and beg her to forgive me for leaving the way I did. I should have fought for her, for us. I follow her with my hungry eyes as she takes the seat nearest my desk. She crosses her ankles and cups her hands on her lap. I want the wild-child Harlow back. However, my eyes land on her tanned legs and move upward. I would love to bend her over my desk and pull that tight skirt up to her waist and… That always happens when she's near.

Her eyes become serious, but the tic of her clasped hands tells me she's nervous. "I've been doing some thinking, and if the position for the Duchess of Ainsworth is still available, I'd like to apply."

My heart races as I comprehend that she's come for me. "I see. Yes, the position is still unfilled, but may I ask why you feel you are the right woman for the job?" I ask, but there could be no other.

She nods and sits up even straighter. "There are several reasons, Your Grace. First, I would be very loyal and supportive to the duke. Plus, my work ethic is stellar as shown here." She pauses and unsnaps her handbag.

I watch in amazement as she pulls a few papers out and hands them to me. I scan the documents and grin feeling like a proud papa. She did it. "This portfolio looks very impressive, Ms. Davidson. Not everyone can accrue a fortune based on her own talents. I commend you." Her eyes shine brightly at my praise. When our gazes meet, I see how much my words mean to her. I've always known she could do whatever she set her mind to.

She clears her throat and goes back into character. She hands me a few more papers. "And I believe you'll find my past work experience favorable."

I look down at the recommendation letters written by Kaylee and Rachael. My lips twitch as I read Rachael's single short sentence: *Hire her or else.* "These seem to be in order."

Her beautiful, vivid eyes shine brightly as she continues the ruse. "But, most importantly, I feel as if I am the very best candidate for the position because I love the duke with all that I am."

I'm out of my chair in seconds and pull her into my arms, branding her with my lips. My hand runs through her hair, and I hear those offensive hair pins ding as they fall to the floor. I kiss her cheeks, the corner of her eyes, and then move back to savor her lips. I growl when she leans back and takes her sweet taste from me.

Her chest rises and falls, and with a teasing glint in her eyes, she asks, "Does this mean I have the job?"

I cup her face in my hands and gaze deeply into her eyes. "There is no one else I would even consider as my duchess. I love you, Harlow Davidson. I can't go another minute, another second without you by my side. I love you with everything that I am. My love, will you marry me?"

Happy tears run down her cheeks as she answers, "Yes. Yes. Yes."

I scoop her up into my arms and carry her from my office. "Mr. Bingham, please call for my driver and cancel all my afternoon appointments."

"Right away, sir," he calls, and I hear his laughter as we go through the door.

Harlow giggles at his reaction. "Where are we going?" she asks as the elevator doors close.

"First, I'm going to make you come on my fingers in the car just to watch your beautiful face glow with pleasure. Then, once we get to Ainsworth Hall, I'm going to take my time and kiss and love every inch of your body, making you come at least three more times before I sink deep inside you. And then we'll do it all again."

"Confident, are you?" the little minx asks with a snide grin.

"I can promise that, by the time I'm through with you, there will be no question of how much I love you and need you in my life." She whimpers, and my cock strains at the zipper.

She pulls her lust-filled eyes to mine and slays me when she says, "That's so hot."

Perfect. This incredible woman is my perfect duchess.

CHAPTER EIGHTEEN

Harlow

Later that evening, as I stand beside Duke in one of the many beautiful rooms of Ainsworth Hall, the woman I've not been looking forward to seeing walks in. Our eyes meet in a standoff. I never thought I'd see her again, but I'm back, and this time I'm staying. My muscles tense as I prepare for the fight of my life. Show no weakness. That mantra repeats in my mind.

"I'd heard you were here," she says from just inside the room.

My chin juts a bit higher. "Yes, ma'am." I turn to Duke and ask, "Would you mind if I have a private chat with your mother?"

He looks me in the eyes and knows I have to do this. "Please?" I say softly.

Reluctantly, he nods. "Of course. I'll go in to dinner and await your arrival." He pecks my lips in a much-too-brief kiss and then gives his mom a pleading look as he walks past. Once he closes the door, we turn and face off.

"Harlow, I hope—"

I stop her with a raised hand. "Just a minute. I get to talk first."

Her lips close into a tight line, and she nods. "Of course. Please do."

I clasp my hands together in front of me and then realize what I'm doing and let them fall to my sides. I am fierce. I can do this. "You were not very nice to me when I was a visitor in your home. I know that you will never approve of me as your son's wife, but you should know that he has asked me to marry him, and I have accepted. Oliver loves you. But he loves me, too. It would hurt him if the two women in his life can't get along. I'm willing to forget the past and start over. You should also know that I am expecting your first grandchild. I don't want any shadows cast about the parentage of our child, so if you require a paternity test, I will gladly allow that." I wait and watch, curious as to what her reaction will be. I see so much in her eyes, but nothing that I understand.

She takes a few steps closer and asks, "Oliver doesn't know, does he?"

I shake my head. "No. Not because I'm keeping it from

him; I just haven't had an opportunity to tell him." I feel my face heat. Duke made good on every promise he'd made in his office. We barely had time to dress for dinner. "Things have been moving rather fast since I got here."

She smiles fondly. "I remember those days. May I speak now?" she asks politely.

I nod and blink at her warm transformation, but I brace myself and wait for her next move.

"Before you showed up today, Oliver and I had a discussion about you. He made me realize that love should be the only consideration when choosing his duchess. He loves you, Harlow. I owe you an apology. I am sorry for making you feel unwelcome and inadequate. I hope you can forgive me, and I would like the opportunity to start over. It's more than I deserve. You've made my son very happy, and you'll always have my trust and support."

I want to look around and see if there are cameras and people ready to jump out and yell 'surprise,' when she takes my hands and kisses my cheek. "You should also know that I've already made plans to move to the Dowager house, so I will not be underfoot."

"You're moving out?" I ask. That had never been my intention. Duke loves his mom, and Ainsworth Hall is huge.

She smiles sadly and nods. "Yes, I feel that's best."

I've been strong until that moment, and my raging hormones cause me to sob and grasp her hands like a lifeline. "But I have no mother, and I want you in my life to help me, to teach me how to be a duchess and how to raise a child as loving, caring, and giving as your son. I want our child to know his or her grandmother." I'm a sniffling mess by the time I finish.

Tears fill her stunned eyes. "I never expected—" She stops, too moved to continue.

"For me. For Oliver. For our child. Please stay." I never expected our conversation to take this turn, but it warms my heart that it did.

CHAPTER NINTEEN

Duke

"My wife is where?" I ask, as I stare down her assistant.

"The Rose Garden, Your Grace," the timid little woman answers.

I pinch the bridge of my nose. I knew she was a stubborn, frustrating woman when I married her, so I have nobody to blame but myself. I sigh then put my hands on my hips and shift my stance. Who am I kidding? I wouldn't have it any other way.

"And what is she doing in the Rose Garden, Ms. Williams?" I work to keep the ire from my voice. Harlow hired the woman without knowing one whit about her. She'd found her outside a fundraiser she'd been hosting and thought she looked hungry and cold. A week later, I find she's my wife's new assistant. Again, I knew this about my wife.

"She's giving a speech for Hope House, sir, at a fundraising luncheon," she says, her voice growing quieter through the last part of the sentence.

My temper rises to the boiling stage. "And why was I not informed about this? It isn't showing on my calendar."

She nods slowly and explains, "That would be because Harlow—I mean, the duchess—requested you not be informed. I believe she said, 'What he doesn't know, he can't put a damper on.'" She giggles then bows her head as she realizes whom she's speaking to.

Oh, she did, did she? I turn and storm down the halls. My wife is going to put me in an early grave. Since before we married, the people of our country have been clamoring for her to make appearances, give speeches, or to back fundraisers for so many different causes that I finally had to put my foot down. She was running herself ragged while trying to please everyone and keep up with her jewelry designs. Not to mention being pregnant. But this? I growl under my breath. She's nine months pregnant and is supposed to be taking it easy.

I push open the double doors to the back patio, make a sharp left, and walk under the pergola where we held our wedding. I never thought I'd live to see the day that Mum agreed to nix the church wedding in favor for a small, quickly arranged, intimate gathering on our estate grounds.

The drama that stirred up in the media was ridiculous, but it helped to endear my wife to the people. Now garden weddings have become popular.

I round the corner and find my beautiful wife standing behind a podium, addressing several dozen well-dressed, influential business men and women. Hope House is her creation and will help numerous homeless individuals get back on their feet with a hand up instead of a hand out. I knew this fundraiser was important to her, but I thought we'd agreed to reschedule it until after the baby is born.

My wife takes my breath away. She's been simply glowing throughout the pregnancy. Well, at least since the morning sickness subsided. She's wearing a blue-and-white print dress, and the sweetheart neckline emphasizes her larger breasts. My cock twitches; I've spent many wondrous hours appreciating those assets. She's standing at least two feet from the microphone, as the large baby bump prevents her from moving closer.

As I stand in the back and watch her work her magic on the crowd, I can't believe my luck in finding the love of my life. I'm one lucky chap that she picked me. She has her hair pinned up today with her graceful, creamy neck showing. I would have missed it if I hadn't been leering after my wife, but I notice her brows draw slightly together in discomfort. Now I watch her more closely and see her hand move several times to her back. When I see her fingers grip the wooden podium, I wait no longer.

Walking to the front of the assembly, I take my wife's

hand. I am somewhat mollified by her remorseful look. However, I do not buy it. I pin her with my eyes before I turn to the guests. "Excuse me. If I may interrupt, the duchess will be leaving now. We would like to thank you for attending and donating to such a worthy cause. Please enjoy the rest of the day's festivities. Good day." With that, I scoop my wife up and head back toward the house.

"Duke, put me down." Harlow says through gritted teeth, yet smiling at everyone we pass.

I don't stop, and I don't slow down. I do, however, feel much calmer with her in my arms. "Duchess, if you know what's good for you, I suggest you keep that lovely mouth closed."

She sighs and rests her head on my shoulder. "Fine. But I don't think you should take me to our bedroom."

"Oh, really? Where would you suggest I take you?" I look down at her and raise my brow. This isn't up for debate.

She smiles much too sweetly up into my eyes. My heart nearly stops when I see a teasing sparkle in her gaze just before she says, "To the hospital. My water broke, and I've been having contractions all morning. But we raised over a million dollars today."

EPILOGUE

"Deep breath in, dear."

I cut my eyes to Mum and open my mouth to tell her my exact opinion about breathing, but then she goes and says, "Now, is that any way for a duchess to act?" She offers more ice chips, but I snap my mouth shut when I feel another contraction coming.

I grit my teeth through the pain and say, "Maybe not, but right now I'm trying to push a baby out of a place that will never be the same again. Breathing doesn't help. Ice doesn't help. I swear I will not let your son within ten feet of me ever again."

Mum bites her lip to keep from laughing. My eyes become slants until the next contraction hits, then I tighten my grip on her hand and focus on her coaching me through the pain. My husband should be in here, but he keeps fainting. The wimp.

I'm panting as I feel the contraction lessen.

"There now, isn't that lovely? Have a bit of a rest now." I'm too exhausted to even think of a snarly comeback.

A nurse comes in to check my progress and increase the meds in my epidural, which I'm eternally grateful for. "Is my husband doing all right?" I ask, smiling as I feel the tension in my body relax.

The nurse chuckles. "Yes, the doctor on call was able to stitch his chin up nicely. Shouldn't even leave a scar. He's asking if he can come back in, but the doctor doesn't recommend it."

I look at Mum, and we laugh. "Oliver's father wasn't in attendance at his birth," she says.

Then I frown and blink my eyes as they fill with tears. "But I really want him with me," I croak, my voice raspy from my sudden onslaught of tears.

Mum hands me a tissue and brushes my hair back from my sweaty forehead. "I understand. Let me see what I can do."

Mum smiles back at me as she goes out the door. In five minutes, she's back with my very remorseful husband. I try not to grin at the bandage on his handsome face. I shouldn't find humor in his inability to see me in pain. It's sweet, really.

I feel a contraction coming and reach my hand out. Duke takes it in his and leans over and kisses my temple. "I love you, Duchess."

His touch calms me as I pant like a dog through the peak

of the contraction. "I know. That's what got us into this in the first place."

His mum snickers from the other side of the bed, which Duke doesn't seem to appreciate. He jumps right into coaching me, with only a mild sweat breaking out on his upper lip.

"Your dad has arrived," Duke tells me, and I feel my tears returning. Duke put my dad up in an apartment near his rehab center when his stay was over. He'd flown Dad and his counselor over for the wedding as a surprise. My dad got to walk me down the aisle. My real dad, not the one he'd become after Mom died. We're working on rebuilding our relationship. It's going to take time, but I'm hopeful.

"Thank you for flying him over," I say and hug his arm, the only part of him I can reach with my stomach being the size of a small elephant.

He leans over, kisses my temple, and I relax even more.

"I told him he has a plane at his disposal anytime he wants to visit," he said.

"Oh, Duke. Thank you. That means so much. Are the girls still here?" I ask.

His brow rises, and his expression takes on a very agitated look. "Humph."

I roll my eyes and look heavenward. "Duke, what happened?" I say in a stern voice.

His lower lip looks like it's getting ready to form a pout, and I want to laugh so bad, but if I do, my whole stomach will shake, and that will set off the monitor alarm.

"Your friends laughed at me," he says indignantly.

"About your little…" I snicker and point to his chin. His mum covers her mouth and giggles.

His eyes narrow, and his lips thin into a tight line as he glares at us both. "Yes. But at least Kyle and Elias could relate. They've been coaching me."

"Oh, heavens," I say, chuckling.

"Oh, and Ms. Edna and Ms. Blanche said they brought enough fruit punch to toast the baby's birth." He winks and grins.

I grasp his arm and pull him down closer and whisper. "Please, don't let your mother have any. In fact, you shouldn't let your mom be unsupervised around them while they're here. You remember what happened at the wedding." I shift my innocent eyes toward her and see her grinning.

We laugh and, sure enough, the baby's monitor goes off, and two nurses run into the room. And we still laugh.

Less than an hour later, tears fill my weary eyes as I look upon my husband holding our tiny son in his arms. Our eyes connect, and we smile. My heart, my life, has never been so full. "I love you, Duke," I say, my voice heavy with exhaustion.

"I love you, Duchess. Are you ready for the ride of our lifetime?"

I smile up into his loving eyes and reply, free from doubts and insecurities, "With you…I wouldn't miss a single second."

Ready for more Love at White Oaks? Up next...
Click here to download Hothead
Or visit LizScottBooks.com for retailer links then keep
reading for
Mastermind's Behind the Book Stuff.

SMITH
I shine in the ER.
I'm in charge.
I flourish in the chaos.
It's who I am,
Where I belong.

But when she walks in,
Everything changes,
I no longer have control,
I'm spiraling into Baylee World,
And all I want is to save her.
Little did I know, she doesn't need to be saved.

She may be a little loony,
A little quirky,
But the only female anatomy this physician is interested in
Is hers.

BAYLEE

When he enters my world,
He makes me believe I can do anything,
At all.

He's smart, sexy, and irresistible.
His faith and encouragement give me strength,
Lets me have courage in myself,
For the first time ever.

But when he breaks me,
I realize what everyone warned me all about,
Never fall for a hothead doctor.

Each book in this small-town hot romance series can be read as a standalone, but for a richer reading experience, the following order is recommended:

Heartbreaker – April & Elias
Troublemaker – Rachael & Kyle
Mastermind – Harlow & Duke
Hothead – Baylee & Smith

BEHIND THE BOOK STUFF

Here's where I get to let loose with behind-the-book stuff you might like to know. This is raw, unedited, and straight from me.

Did you put Harlow's name together? I like to have fun with names. Sometimes I'm the only one that gets it, but I still get my grins and giggles just knowing. Harlow's dad called her Harley and their last name is Davidson. Sooo...

Several of the characters in Mastermind were named by readers in my Facebook Readers Group! Duke's name was going to be Oliver Phillip Ainsworth, but a reader suggested to throw another name in, so he became Oliver Alexander Phillip Ainsworth. That sounds much more royal, don't you think?

Duke was originally going to be a Baron, but a reader suggested to go all out and let him be a Duke. Which worked into the name misunderstanding. I did research British titles. I think my Duke would fit in nicely.

When I first came up with this series, Duke and I had already met. He was already going to be the third book of the series, but I never could decide on who was going to be his forever after. Harlow came to me while I was writing Troublemaker. I kept seeing a woman stranded at a hotel near White Oaks. It took me weeks before I knew what happened to her. Then everything just fell into place.

Creating Tea Charms was a happy accident! I am a tea drinker, and I frequently find myself digging the tea tag from my cup. I have often wished there was something to keep that darn tag on the outside. When Harlow had the same problem...ta da! Tea Charms was created! I had so much fun with this. The more I thought about it, I decided to see if I could make some. They would make a great give-away. So, I did, and they are so cute and I have some original handmade by me tea charms for sale in my store at LizScottBooks.com.

Update: A reader burst my bubble when she told me she bought tea jewelry when she was in Ireland years ago. So, I guess my tea charms aren't so original after all. Bummer. But they are still cute!

The next book in this series will be Hothead. You've already met Baylee. Are you curious? Did you already fall in love with her? I certainly have.

Join our Private Lizabeth Scott Readers Group on Facebook, where I'm always sharing behind-the-book stuff. Oh, and for updates on releases, giveaways, and special announcements join my Newsletter Community by clicking HERE or join by going to LizScottBooks.com

And lastly, but most important, if you enjoyed Heartbreaker, please leave a short review on the retailer where you purchased the book to help others find my books.

Please keep in touch! I'd love to hear from you. You can find out more about me and my books on my website: LizScottBooks.com.

YOU MIGHT LIKE

The Royal Vow Series

Sweet Royal Beginnings

Sweet Surrender

Sweet Denial

Sweet Seduction

Sweet Temptation

Sweet Destiny

Hearts of Gold Series

A Sheik for Rose

A Star for Annie

A Cowboy for Mary

Dirty Ankle Series

You Promised Me Forever

Kissed Series

Snow Kissed by the Billionaire

Chased by the Billionaire

Sun Kissed by the Billionaire

French Kissed by the Billionaire

Connect with Liz on

Website: LizScottBooks.com

Facebook: LizabethScottAuthor

Twitter: @LScottBooks

Instagram: lizabethscottauthor

BookBub: bookbub.com/authors/lizabeth-scott

GoodReads:
goodreads.com/author/show/8122729.Lizabeth_Scott

For updates on releases, giveaways,

and special announcements

join my Newsletter Community by clicking

HERE or join by going to LizScottBooks.com

ABOUT THE AUTHOR

Lizabeth spent years doing extensive research in preparation for writing her own stories by reading every romance book she could get her hands on. At least that's how she justifies her HUGE collection of romance books to Mr. Scott.

Liz grew up on a dairy farm in western North Carolina where she wrote her first story at the age of thirteen about her first love...horses. She married her high school sweetheart and they have 2 children and 2 simply adorable grands. With her children now settled and on their own Liz pulled her dreams of writing back out and that little spark that sizzled for years caught fire and is now roaring back to life.

Liz loves to read and write stories about quirky, endearing heroines and the strong, handsome heroes who love them to distraction. She promises you a few laughs along the way with some steamy and charming moments thrown in but always a happy ever after.